AN ALIEN STORM

CALLA ZAE

PROSE CONCEPTS

AN ALIEN STORM

SOLDIERS OF SAEDO 4

CALLA ZAE

COPYRIGHT

An Alien Storm

Copyright © 2021 by Calla Zae

Cover Art Copyright: Calla Zae

Space Map Art Copyright: Calla Zae

All rights reserved. Published by Prose & Concepts LLC.

No part of this book may be reproduced or transmitted in any form or by any means, electronic, or mechanical, including photocopying, recording, or by any information storage and retrieval system without written permission from the publisher. For information:

Prose & Concepts LLC

210 Park Avenue, Suite #280

Worcester, MA 01609

www.proseandconcepts.com

This book is a work of fiction. All characters, places, names, and events are a product of the author's imagination. Any resemblance to events, locations, or persons alive or otherwise, is entirely coincidental.

First edition Ebook ISBN: 978-1-952820-11-3

First edition Paperback ISBN: 978-1-952820-17-5

Audiobook ISBN: 978-1-952820-12-0

ALARUS GALAXY MAP
PLANET CELERON

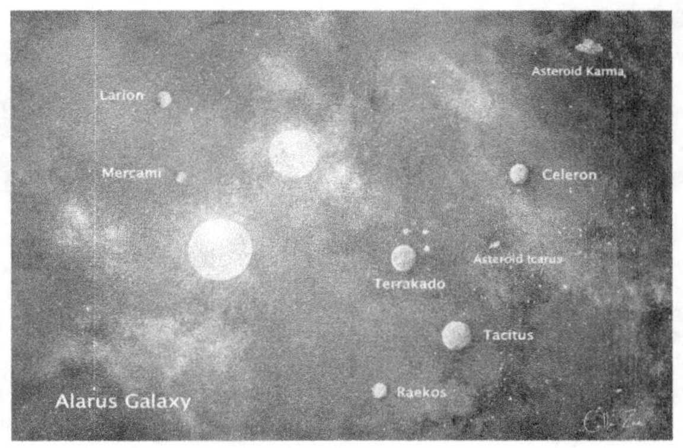

ONE

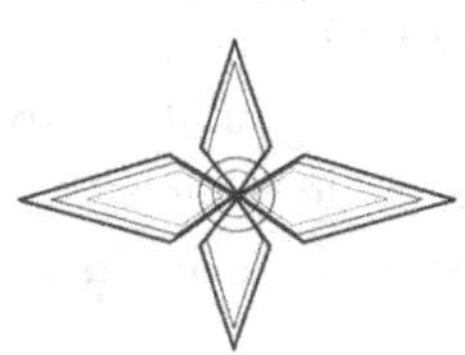

Vanessa clutched her stomach as she sat inside Sasha's state-of-the-art home. She curled on a couch made of high-tech fabric that changed scenic views at random. Despite the peaceful landscapes, the erratic nerves remained and settled at the center of her gut, radiating out to her entire body. Her stomach tightened, and an uncomfortable sensation she hadn't felt before squirmed through her, and she shuddered from the tingles.

"You okay there?" Sasha asked, offering a cup of herbal tea with a layer of stars sparkling over the liquid. The dream plant was supposed to induce a good night's sleep, which Vanessa desperately needed.

Living in the Province of Saedo on planet Celeron had opened Vanessa's eyes to an abundance of plants that enabled her to create the most interesting culinary dishes she could ever imagine.

Vanessa took the warm cup, leaning in to inhale the sweet steam. "Thank you. I don't know what's going on with my stomach lately." Was it a stomach issue or something else? She didn't want to worry her six siblings, so she kept the details to herself for now. "Maybe I've been experimenting with too much food at work, and the combination isn't working out well for my stomach?"

"The Happy Belly has been busy with all the dishes you've created. Abba must be excited for all the business." Inga sat down beside her and crossed her legs.

Vanessa used her culinary skills to spice up the menu with some human flair. The Saedo villagers responded well, and that delighted Abba, the owner. Her profits had tripled from Vanessa's creations.

Vanessa learned that certain ingredients could create chemical imbalances, so maybe that was why her stomach was upset. However, intuition told her differently. She sipped the tea and the sparkling steam tingled her tongue. For the past three days, she'd been dreaming about her ex-husband, Travis. She didn't know why he'd come back into her thoughts now. Their relationship had ended over a year ago. But then again, the ghost of an abusive relationship followed her no matter where she went. Even on a new planet.

He wasn't here, was he? The thought chilled her, and she shivered.

"Are you sure you're not coming down with something?" Inga wrapped an arm around Vanessa.

Inga had just moved into Osayik's house last week, and the loving energy radiated from the couple wherever they went. Just over a week ago, Inga and Osayik battled Ulkrin creatures including a mother beast that spoke the universal language, which Vanessa also understood from the language translator inside her ear. She could read the universal language after a doctor activated the language codex within her brain via a beam of energy. The human brain was a magical wonder that hadn't been fully discovered yet.

What other threats were coming to Saedo? This odd churning in her gut warned her to be careful, or was it just discomfort from food aversion? Vanessa was a chef and food was her specialty, so she should be used to all kinds of food by now. But she was on a new planet. She convinced herself that was the reason for the stomach issues.

Inga leaned in and ran her fingers down a lock of Vanessa's red hair. "You're the only one with red hair. Are you sure you're our sister?"

All her siblings had inherited the brown except her. Somehow, she came out different from the rest of the family. Her mom mentioned Vanessa was blessed with the fire from one of her great-great-grandmothers, who was a priestess from back in the day. She didn't know if it was true or just something the family made up to make her feel better. Vanessa didn't care, she embraced her fire... until her damn husband snuffed it out.

Her silence earned a tug on her hair.

"Only a real sister could deal with you." Vanessa elbowed Inga and answered the other question. "I don't think I'm coming down with anything. Extra sleep would probably help."

"Take a few days off from work," Sasha suggested. "That fire in you is coming back. Saedo is truly helping us become our best selves."

There was no need to mention that Travis had invaded her dreams. His name would infuriate them, remind them all of what he had done to her. Her body remembered and wanted to shudder, but she willed herself to be strong and not give him any more power.

Her sisters didn't need to worry about her now. She was fine. She just needed to rest. That was all.

Vanessa glanced at the time on her smart pendant, dangling from the gold chain. "Where is everybody?"

For tonight, the seven sisters planned a girls' night out at Sasha's huge house that her lover, Maeson, had built. Grandma Ova agreed to stop by for a discussion about Saedo lore.

"Rita won't be able to make it. She's helping with the renovations at the Village Library. Emma, Isabella, and Nina already can't make it either. So it's just Sasha, me, and you. It was a last-minute idea, anyway." Inga made herself a fruit bowl. "Thanks for hosting us, Sasha. Your massive house is the only one that can host all of us at once, and your backyard has the best view of the stars."

"Anything for my sisters. Besides, I'm curious to know what Grandma has to share about Saedo lore. She should be here any minute." Sasha checked her smart ring. "She only lives up the street."

"She's probably bringing a pot of her herbal soup for us," Vanessa said. No one in Saedo could resist Grandma Ova's soup, which was a blend of herbs and vegetables from her abundant gardens. She prayed a bowl of that soup would settle her stomach.

At first, Vanessa thought about cancelling to go home and sleep, but curiosity won out. Saedo lore intrigued her. Emma, Sasha, and Inga had all inspired a rare flower bud to grow after they met their starmates, their forever mates. Each flower reflected the color of their lover's mist. No one else could see it but them.

Would she inspire a flower to grow? Would she ever find her forever mate? Or was she too flawed, too wounded to attract that? She had tossed out her wish to the Universe on that fateful New Year's Eve night when she and her sisters were abducted by the horrible Ulkrins and rescued by the soldiers of Saedo.

I deserve a man who loves me regardless of my wounds.

Though Vanessa's idea of happily ever after had disappeared after Travis, a part of her yearned for the impossible. It was normal to want what you couldn't have, right? This opportunity to delve into Saedo lore allowed her to believe in magic again. When she was younger, she loved getting tarot card readings even though she couldn't tell if they were true. But they gave her hope, and hope saved her sanity.

The doorbell chimed, and Sasha rushed over and opened the door.

"Hi, Grandma Ova! The gang's all here for you. Come on in. Here, let me take that." Sasha grabbed the large pot in the elderly woman's hands and placed it on the dining table. "Make yourself at home."

Grandma Ova's white hair gleamed silver against her light green skin. "I'm so happy to see all of you. I've been meaning to go down to the Village Center and meet everyone, but once my injured legs healed, there were too many administrative things I needed to catch up on." She embraced Inga and Vanessa.

From Sasha, Vanessa learned that Grandma Ova was one thousand and three hundred solar cycles old. But her vibrant eyes, smooth skin, and healthy white hair portrayed her as someone in their early sixties. She was told that time behaved differently on this planet, even though a solar cycle was similar to one year on Earth. Most of all, it was the energy that made the lifestyle different. She learned that Earth vibrated on a third dimensional matrix as opposed to planet Celeron, which existed on an eighth dimensional matrix. The higher vibrations affected how the bodies and cells reacted to aging. Vanessa didn't understand it all, but she concluded these star-beings lived a long life.

Would her lifespan be like theirs too?

After everyone had a bowl of soup, they gathered in the living room with a huge skylight. Vanessa's stomach settled a bit. Sasha slid the side door open, and a sweet breeze snuck in.

"What's that lovely scent?"

Grandma Ova smiled, pointing toward the pink grass field. The tips of the grass glittered like gems as they swayed. "When the suns go down for the evening, the spade of the grass opens and releases a sweet fragrance. During the day, they collect the rays of the sun and make this sweet substance that they share during the evening."

"What's all the glitter on it?" Vanessa inquired.

Grandma Ova's amber eyes warmed. "It's a sparkle they show off at night. They're like stars. The sweet fragrance has healing properties. So inhale it, it'll release tension in your muscles. I usually tell people to camp outside for a night near a field of pink grass to heal any muscle ailments."

The wonders of this planet continued to awe Vanessa. Nature was truly healing, and the villagers appreciated their land.

Grandma Ova sat in a wide armchair with two large pillows. "I understand you girls have questions for me."

Inga and Sasha were curled up on the wide couch, while Vanessa sat on the shaggy rug with a soft pillow in front of her.

"We'd love it if you could tell us anything about the significance of these flowers." Inga pressed her smart bracelet, pulling up a virtual screen that showed the three flower buds. The yellow bud from Emma's garden was still closed, but hers had more leaves sprouting around it. Sasha's blue bud and Inga's red bud hadn't opened either.

Grandma Ova placed a hand to her heart, which the star-beings referred to as corra. Tears welled in her eyes as she zoomed in on each image. "You don't understand how delighted I am to see this. These are blessings beyond my imagination."

Grandma Ova's hands trembled, and Sasha retrieved a cup of warm herbal tea and offered it. Grandma Ova took the cup, sipped, and looked at the sisters. "I knew something was different the day the soldiers brought you here. The energy shifted. I felt it in my bones. I love this land, and there's so much wonder and magic in it. It is sacred, and when this kind of shift happens, that tells me the land is ready for a change."

Vanessa stared at her, holding on to her every word, like a kid hypnotized by a fairytale.

Grandma Ova continued, "As you already know, each star-being here possesses their own special mist color that only they and their starmate can see. The mist chooses the mate from energy resonance. It knows what's best for each individual. Color is important as well. The magic is in the details, so pay attention to the flowers and the mist. They'll give little hints on what they need you to do."

The concept fascinated Vanessa, and she turned toward the skylight. Was that a shooting star she just saw? She blinked, and it was gone. It was probably an illusion. Magical things like that didn't happen to her.

"Each mist color represents a wave in the color spectrum." Grandma opened her arms for emphasis. "Each wave holds a certain energy, and each energy field has its own purpose. Some we can see, some we can't."

"It sounds complicated," Vanessa said. There was a point in time when she used to love dissecting the meanings behind meanings, but after her failed marriage, she stopped looking for the hidden meanings. However, right now, in this moment, something dormant sparked in her again. The desire to believe in magic sprouted in her.

Was that the reason for all the nerves?

"Everything is perspective, my dear. If you learn how to look through the right lenses, everything will have a divine meaning to it." Grandma Ova looked at her with keen interest.

"We were destined to be in Saedo," Sasha said. "It's bizarre, but everything seems to point that way."

"The Cosmos is extraordinary and powerful. It has plans for all of us—the planets, the inhabitants, all the worlds and dimensions. It's mind-blowing, and there's a beauty to witnessing what happens and trust that the outcome is for your benefit." She pointed to the images of the flower buds. "Love gave birth to these flowers for a reason. These are called blessiums. It's been eons since I've seen them. The last time they grew, they saved a star race from being destroyed."

Inga gasped. "What?"

"That sounds serious," Sasha muttered.

"It is," Grandma Ova said. "I know about the story because my friend and her family were the recipients of the flowers' blessings. There were three buds then as well, and this occurred in another province, so these flowers don't belong to a particular territory. They belong to the Cosmos, and they are here for a reason. Something is happening here in Saedo, and I have a feeling more flowers will emerge."

Vanessa's heart thudded for no reason. The powerful pounding made the nerves in her stomach appear like a whisper. "Do you think Saedo is in danger?"

Grandma Ova pressed her lips into a thin line. "I think something is trying to disrupt Saedo, and these flowers will help fight it." She looked at all the sisters and her gaze landed on Vanessa. "All of you are part of it. It was meant to be. You were meant to be here in this now moment."

A hint of fear and uncertainty flashed across Sasha and Inga's faces. The same emotion stirred in Vanessa.

Grandma Ova noticed it. "I don't mean to frighten you. I just wanted to tell you the truth. The truth can be scary, but the fear will dissipate once you understand it. Knowing ahead of time only prepares you. Love is the most potent energy in the Cosmos. It's a pure energy that transcends time and space. Love made these flowers, and that means we have the most powerful energy as our ally."

"What do you think is happening in Saedo?" Vanessa asked.

Grandma Ova lifted a shoulder. "I didn't pick up on

anything during my meditations. Sometimes I learn things from the land, and sometimes from the sky. Spirit is always guiding us. We must pay attention and listen. Right now, what I'm feeling is that we need to wait and watch." Her chin gestured to the night sky. "Have you noticed something odd in the sky this past week?"

"The dark clouds," Inga said. "They seemed strange because the suns are still shining while these dark clouds are hanging in the air. I mean, I understand weather is strange and you can have dark clouds on a sunny day, but they look... stiff, stagnant, and out of place to me."

Inga with her love for fashion and the arts would notice small details like that.

"Yes, you're right. Those clouds have a strange energy to them. I've been watching them too. They seem to disappear during certain times of the day and then reappear. For instance, right now, I don't see them, which is why we can see the stars clearly. Keep an eye on them. Maybe they're just normal clouds signifying an impending storm."

"I started seeing them a week ago, but there hasn't been a storm in Saedo yet. Is there something we should be doing?" Inga asked.

"No, the village weather forecast will alert us if the radars pick up something dangerous. Like I said, these are speculations based on my knowledge of things. I could be wrong."

Vanessa didn't believe that.

"I'm sharing this information with you because you have an interest in Saedo stories," Grandma Ova said. "And like all stories, there are lessons to be learned. You carry high vibrational energy, all of you. Saedo loves it, hence the rare flowers, but something isn't used to this energy."

Or doesn't like it. Vanessa had no idea where that thought came from.

"I say we keep tossing these high vibrations in its face." Sasha made a sprinkling gesture.

Inga pounded a clenched fish to her palm. "That's right. Anyone or anything that wants to destroy love deserves to be crushed like garlic. Right, Vanessa?"

"Smashed, chopped, and completely destroyed. Nothing messes with the Nelson sisters." Vanessa made a chopping motion with her hand.

Grandma Ova beamed. "That's exactly what I'm talking about. You raise the vibration from your joy and intention. I think you've heard enough about Saedo lore for tonight. I have to get going. I need to wake up early and prepare a few things for the two assistants I hired to help me with my gardens."

After Grandma Ova left for the evening, Sasha and Maeson went to bed. Inga took one of the guest rooms. Vanessa could hear her chatting with her love, Osayik, who was on a business trip with Chief Mozar. Vanessa chose the comfortable sectional so she could gaze up at the night sky. She pressed the button on the wall, and the skylight opened. A sea of stars mesmerized her.

As Vanessa immersed herself in the wonder of it all, the nerves in her stomach resurfaced like a wave of remembrance, making her shudder. What was happening to her body?

She prayed for a restful night because she needed the energy to get through work tomorrow.

TWO

After a restless night, Vanessa yearned for a day off. But she couldn't do that to Abba. Abba hired Vanessa to work with her at the Happy Belly restaurant when she settled in the Main Village, which was about the size of a large suburb. The Province of Saedo was comprised of several villages, and Vanessa and her sisters resided in the main one. They worked in the Village Center, which was like the downtown area of any city. It was packed with shops and activities.

Happy Belly had three family parties scheduled for today, and Vanessa's assistance, along with two other star-being chefs, was vital to the day's success. She loved her work; it kept her mind busy, so she didn't have to think about the dream from last night. Why was Travis reappearing in her mind? She had no feelings for him other than disappointment. She should hate him for the scars he left on her body, for the trauma that seeped into her bones. But all she felt was disappointment and pity. Was that wrong of her?

Travis was a lost soul who could never understand love or any kind of positive affection. It took her a long time to see that.

She remembered how she'd fallen head over heels for his charm, but that was just a front for the monster within.

The burn scar that ran along her arm twitched as if it remembered what the skillet had done. The muscle on her shoulder throbbed as it relived the moment he shoved her against the bookcase.

She closed her eyes, squeezing away those dreadful memories. *Go away! Leave me alone.*

Vanessa opened her eyes as a stream of sweat slid from her forehead down the side of her face. It dripped onto her uniform which consisted of a peach top and black pants. She wiped another bead of sweat on her sleeve as she dropped into the chair in the backroom.

"You look beat. Take a break. We've got this." Abba prepared a plate of food for the customers waiting in front of the restaurant. She had three eyes, purple hair, dark green skin, and a warm smile that made everyone feel welcome. Her mother watched her young children while she worked at the restaurant. Her husband left her last solar cycle for another star-being with a bigger bust.

Vanessa blew out a breath. "I didn't sleep too well last night."

"It's been crazy busy, and I'm not complaining, but you've been on your feet for six hours without a break. I don't want you passing out on me. I need my best chef recharged so she can continue to help me." The third eye on the side of her forehead winked, while the other two focused on the garnish. "D-1 and D-2 can hold the fort back here."

The humanoid droids stopped loading the Aquajet—a massive dishwasher—with dirty plates and cutlery. They both whirled toward her. "Take a break, Vanessa. We don't want you passing out. We like your presence here."

She smiled at the male and female droids that looked like

brown-skinned star-beings. D-1 was a female with short green hair and D-2 a bald male. Both were programmed to lift heavy things, reach for boxes in high places, clean the floors, wash the dishes, cut the vegetables, and help with anything that their software provided.

Vanessa wished she had one of these droids when she was on Earth. She could program it to help her with whatever she needed. It would save her time. But then again, convenience would probably make her lazy.

"I suppose I can take a break. I can always rely on you both." It still amazed her that she was living, working, and talking to star-beings and droids on another planet. Just months ago, she was living on Earth unsure of what she wanted. Now, she was in Saedo mending her heart and soul, finding her way to who she was before the trauma. These star-beings showed her more kindness than a man who once vowed to love her.

She rose from the chair and glanced outside. Some fresh air would clear her mind and energize her. "Do you need anything from the garden? I'm going to take a short break outside."

Abba looked into her basket. "Some herbs and maybe a few jomatoes. The salads are selling fast this week. Can you get me a combination of colors? Thanks."

"Will do."

Vanessa entered the bathroom and splashed cold water on her face, washing away the sweat. The cold water refreshed her, giving her a boost of energy. Dark circles hung heavy under her eyes. She should have worn some makeup before getting to work, but she had been too tired. Her braid had come undone, and the messy red hair stuck out like a bird's nest.

After fixing her braid, she grabbed a basket and strode out to the back door and into the huge yard that also served as a garden for the restaurant. Farther back lay a wide ditch with a small stream that separated the yard from the woods.

She headed over to the jomatoe bush, which was similar to grape or cherry tomatoes on Earth. But these jomatoes grew in clumps of threes or fours, and they came in various colors. Some even had dots that made them look like ladybugs.

Nature healed in many ways. She inhaled a big breath, held it in her lungs, and released it. Her body lightened a bit, but the nerves lingered at the pit of her belly, causing a minor cramp and tightness in her chest that often occurred from worrying too much. But she wasn't concerned about anything right now. So why were they bothering her? She inhaled another breath, and though the muscles relaxed, energy zapped her. Something hissed like static electricity.

What was this strange sensation?

The unease reminded her of times her body coiled with tension in anticipation of what Travis would find wrong with her that day. Were these nerves warning her about something? Was she developing some kind of syndrome? That was the last thing she needed. What the hell was going on with her? *I need sleep.* Tonight, she'd go home, shower, and go straight to bed.

She held a purple jomatoe in her hand. "It's not too much to ask, right?" She dropped it into the basket. "I just want a good night's sleep. That's not a difficult thing to ask. Everyone needs rest, even you."

If someone were to listen to her talk to her vegetables, they'd consider her insane. She didn't care. Plants were living things too. Just because they couldn't speak didn't mean they weren't alive.

"Sometimes, I wish I could be like you." She glanced down at the pink jomatoe. "Your life is simple, and you exist for one purpose only. You're food to the birds, animals, and the customers who come to Happy Belly. You don't have a dark past you're trying to erase. You don't have nightmares. You just exist—"

"I'm sure it has nightmares too, especially when a giant mouth with big teeth is about to bite into it. Wouldn't that scare you?" a voice sounded from behind her.

She whirled and gasped as a green star-being climbed up from the ditch about twenty feet from her. In one hand, he held a tablet, and in the other, a scanning device that blinked. He surveyed the area, pointed the device at the soil, and glanced back to the tablet. Then he clicked the device off.

He strode up to her. "Sorry I startled you. I didn't mean to eavesdrop. I was working near the ditch and heard a voice."

She recognized him as one of the soldiers who had rescued her and her sisters. The soldiers of Saedo were the elite police force of the province. Besides working with Chief Mozar on government business, most of them had other occupations and interests. Her sisters' lovers contributed to the villages with building construction, cybersecurity on the Galacto Net, which was like a massive internet for the galaxy, city planning, and so much more. They were multitalented, and it intrigued her how they embraced their responsibilities without complaint. The men she'd encountered in her life didn't have the same exuberance as these star-beings who worked so well together. Maybe she never had the opportunity to meet the right man.

"It's okay." She shrugged as a new wave of nerves escalated in her stomach. This sensation differed from the cramping and chest tightening. The excitement reminded her of nerves that emerged when she started a new job or did something thrilling. "I talk to the plants a lot. It's nothing new. I'm Vanessa. You're friends with Raeko, Maeson, and Osayik, right?"

"Yes, they're my brothers. I'm Arkon. We've missed each other a few times at Raeko's house. I've had your pies. They're delicious."

"Oh, thank you."

She did miss a few parties at Emma and Raeko's house.

Emma had fallen in love with Raeko during the rescue mission, and now they were living their happily ever after. Grandma Ova's words popped into her mind.

You were meant to be here in this now moment.

Arkon smiled, and a warmth zapped her skin, skating down her spine. She willed her body to calm. The energy around them slowed, and the gentle breeze that caressed her skin moments ago froze in time. Even the plants stopped swaying, or was that her imagination?

He was a gorgeous green man who stood well over six feet tall with broad shoulders formed from hours in the gym. He wore a short-sleeve black knit top that showed off his taut muscles and high-tech denim pants that defined his strong thighs and legs. He had high cheek bones, a square jaw, and deep-set eyes that pulled her in. His brown hair was tied into a short tail with a leather strap. A sexy mouth with fine lips curved, and for a moment, she wondered what it would feel like to kiss them.

What? Vanessa blinked at the audacity of her fantasies.

Sunlight glittered in his eyes, making his irises appear copper. She should stop staring at him. She should stop being rude. But her brain and her body had other plans that included wild images of him in the nude. The shock of it startled her. When was the last time her body reacted to a man like this? She couldn't remember.

She willed her mind to the present moment and changed the topic. "What were you doing down at the ditch?"

"I'm investigating something for the city. There are unidentifiable holes along the ditch that follow the stream. I'm trying to figure out what's causing them. Have you seen anything out of the ordinary here?" He gestured to the yard.

"No, I don't think so, just the usual plants, birds, and animals. Sometimes I go down to the ditch during my break and watch the birds play in the stream. I haven't noticed anything strange, but I'll keep an eye out for you."

Arkon tapped something on the tablet, and his shiny brass wristband blinked with data codes. His fingers worked fast. When he was done, he looked at her. "Please do. That'd be great. I'll give you my identification."

She clutched her smart pendant and touched it to his wristband, syncing the information.

"Great. Thank you." He smiled and reached a hand toward her, and she flinched with an arm bracing to defend herself.

Arkon retracted his hand. "I'm sorry. I was just going to remove the dried leaf that's stuck in your hair. I wasn't—"

Shame and embarrassment heated her face. "It's okay. It's been a long day. I'm not myself today."

Why did she allow Travis to sneak into her life even on this planet? She refused to give him any power over her. That time was over. It pissed her off that, somehow, his presence still lingered and affected her life. How could she get rid of him? How could she make herself forget the trauma?

The concerned look on Arkon's face beckoned for information. How could she explain this to him?

She didn't know him. She didn't need to tell him anything. That brought her some relief.

His eyes steeled, but his voice was calm. "How did you get the scar on your arm?"

"It's a wound from a long time ago."

"You didn't answer my question."

I don't need to.

He stared at her, and more questions swam in his eyes. She could guess his internal war. The desire to know why she thought he was going to hit her and how she had gotten the scar. But he should understand he was in no position to pry answers out of her. It was none of his business, and she preferred it that way. The past was best left in the past. She didn't want to talk about it.

"Some things aren't meant to be discussed with strangers," Vanessa said as nerves tumbled in her stomach again.

His lips thinned, and he nodded without comment.

"I've got to get back to work." She tightened her grip on the basket of jomatoes. "Like I said, I'll keep an eye out for anything unusual for you."

"Thank you."

With basket in tow, she turned and headed to the door. She knew he was watching her. His gaze singed her back, and her body tingled from the sensation that lingered long after she was inside.

Was her body's reaction a side effect of embarrassment, of him seeing her flaw? Or was it something more?

THREE

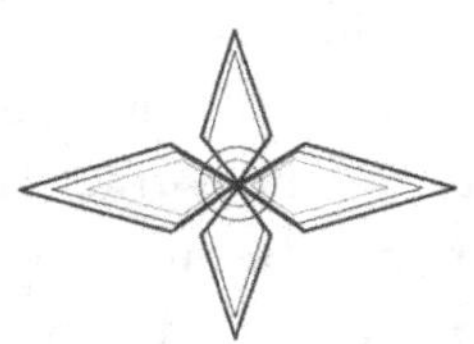

The next day, hungry customers swamped Happy Belly, wanting to try Vanessa's new dish, the Nelson meat pie with a Saedo twist. It was her version of a shepherd's pie. She released it two days ago, and orders kept coming in for pick-ups and deliveries in addition to sit-in dining.

Abba beamed as she checked her daily profits. "I don't normally review numbers in detail like this, but the Nelson meat pies have been such a big hit. Thank you."

"Thank *you* for giving me a job." Vanessa gave Abba a one-arm hug. The villagers had accepted her and her sisters with open arms, giving all of them opportunities to make a decent living.

"Best decision I've ever made. I'm going into my office to make some calls. I'll be back." Abba strode down the hallway to her office.

The front doorbell chimed as more customers stepped in. Vanessa wouldn't have noticed or bothered to look, but an energy slammed into her like it wanted her attention. She glanced up from the counter and noticed Arkon taking a seat facing the back garden.

What was he doing back here? Did he find what was causing those holes in the ditch?

He met her eyes and waved. Vanessa remembered the strange exchange from yesterday. Embarrassment still lingered, so she let Klori, the sage-skinned waitress with curly yellow hair, serve him. Vanessa continued with her inventory list and balanced the numbers on the virtual screen. Numbers and Vanessa weren't on friendly terms. They were too rigid, too analytical, too strict. She preferred something with more flexibility, more creativity. She could never work at a bank or anything that required meticulous concentration. With food, if she were a bit off, it could taste good. With numbers, if she were off by a few digits, chaos would erupt.

Klori stepped up to the counter. "Vanessa, do you know that sexy star-being over there? He keeps looking your way, trying to get your attention, but you're glued to the screen here." She jerked her chin at Arkon. "He's working on something while he's having lunch. He ordered your pie and asked if you could stop by when you get a chance."

Vanessa wasn't trying to avoid him, was she? Who was she kidding? She didn't want him to ask about her scar again. Not only that, there was something about him that made her want to kiss him amongst other decadent things. The wild Vanessa—the one who was shoved into a corner by violence—was finding the courage to get out of that corner. Arkon lured her without having a clue. Did she want to give another man that power? The wanting, the needing, and the curiosity all tangled together in a wild turbulence in her mind. When she looked at him, desire sparked in her.

Was it just repressed sexual energy? Or was it her hormones acting up? She wasn't due for her menstrual cycle for another two months. The herbal pills she'd gotten from Grandma Ova also served as a contraceptive that allowed her body to skip a few cycles.

She learned a while ago that hiding was cowardice. Facing her issues head-on was how to resolve them. She was no coward. It took her a while to understand this, and that was when she finally filed for divorce from Travis. The problems had glared at her from the beginning, but love was blind. When he chased her with a knife and threatened to kill her and her sisters, the blindfold came off. She felt so stupid for being under that dark spell.

No more hiding.

When the order for the Nelson meat pie came, she brought it over to Arkon. From his brass wristband, he pulled up two small screens in front of him while he sipped a fruit shake.

"You're a busy man." Vanessa set down the plate decorated with edible flowers.

He smiled and sniffed. "I've heard rave reviews about this pie." He took a fork, dove in, and made a sound that sent a jolt to her core. "I think I need to order two more of them for dinner."

Vanessa laughed, and the awkwardness that had been there yesterday vanished. "Klori said you had some questions for me?"

"Yes. I was just wondering if you've seen anything strange by the ditch."

"No, I haven't been back out there." She studied his screens. Numbers, charts, graphs, and neat summaries splashed on two screens. "You like numbers? You like to analyze things with an absolute answer?"

He pinned her with an inquisitive look. "I like to know exactly where things fall. I don't like to leave things to chance. I make my own solution based on facts. Sometimes, I make an educated guess based on data I've collected."

What did you collect about me?

"I'm the opposite. I don't like things with one definite answer.

I like limitless things, things that could have many possibilities. Kind of like my recipes. I can create something from anything. There's no one way of doing it, and I can have many solutions."

His lips twisted as he seemed to consider her words. "That's a compelling perspective. I've always been good with data and research. I know where those details will lead me, and I can anticipate the outcome. I tried to do things differently a long time ago, and that failed miserably. You're the creative type, so you wouldn't like numbers. I don't have a creative bone in me." He paused and studied her. "We are different."

"We're opposite each other."

"No, we're polarities."

Vanessa arched an eyebrow. She hadn't heard that explanation before.

"In simple terms, we exhibit energies that complement each other. Together, they complete each other. Like inhaling and exhaling, night and day. They are 'opposites,' yet they complete the entire process."

"That's an interesting way of looking at it." The longer she stood near him, the more her body warmed. "Well, you enjoy your meal. I've got to get back to work. I'll be sure to let you know if I see something in the ditch."

Did something happen last night to make him think she saw something in the ditch today? He didn't seem concerned. Then it occurred to her. Did he come to Happy Belly just to talk to her? No, that couldn't be it. Could it? It had been so long since any man showed interest in her. The truth was that she hadn't been open to dating then. But now, she wanted to know. It had been so long that she'd forgotten how it worked.

Arkon turned heads with the female star-beings. He could date any star-being in Saedo. Was he with anyone? That thought didn't even cross her mind until now.

Vanessa entered the back room and assisted the food orders with Klori and Bashlin, the waitress with the long, dark hair.

Her heart raced as Arkon's face popped into her vision. Why couldn't she push him out of her mind? This powerful attraction gripped her senseless. She hardly knew him. Why would a man like him want anything to do with a simple human female like her? She had a darkness that still haunted her. Being with her meant he had to deal with those monsters too. Who would want the extra baggage?

Despite all those thoughts, his exquisite face and mesmerizing copper eyes did strange things to her stomach. A different set of nerves churned, and for a moment, a spark of hope brought a smile to her face. There was nothing wrong with imagination. She could have a private story unfolding in her mind about him. No one had to know.

Time flew by as more customers arrived and kept Vanessa on her toes.

"I'll see you tomorrow." Klori waved at Vanessa, who was opening a bag of plant-based napkins.

"Already?" Vanessa checked her smart pendant and blinked. Five hours passed by in a blink. She glanced over where Arkon had sat, but he wasn't there. Of course, he wasn't there. Did she think he'd sit there all day waiting to talk to her? He had come in for lunch, and that was it. Would he come back tomorrow?

A twinge of disappointment settled in. It was better that way. She didn't need Arkon to complicate her perfect lifestyle. She worked, went home, experimented on her secret recipe collection, and went to bed. One day, she'd have her own restaurant with the freedom to create whatever she pleased. Happy Belly allowed her the liberty to explore, but it wasn't her restaurant. Vanessa wanted something that represented every aspect of her.

At a glance, her life sounded boring, but she was content. She didn't have to worry about the verbal abuse that came from a wrong word choice, or from the incorrect way she greeted anyone. *Incompetent bitch. Stupid slut.* These were names Travis used to call her in addition to the smacking and punching just because he had a bad day.

She adored her simple life now. Though she would love to connect to a man again, she was afraid. What if he ended up the same as Travis? Her body quaked from that thought.

Stop thinking. Stop analyzing. She had one thing in common with Arkon: she overanalyzed things that should be left alone.

Vanessa blew out a breath as she focused on refilling the napkin rack behind the counter for the takeout orders.

"Long day?" His voice startled her.

Her heart jumped with joy. "Hi. Are you here to pick up an order? I didn't see a pending order on the screen." She searched the screen again.

"No order. I'm here for you. Do you have a minute?" Copper eyes looked at her, and her legs lost their balance.

Vanessa assumed he wanted to ask more questions about the ditch or share some information about his investigation.

"Sure." She gestured for him to follow her through the side door onto the private patio filled with pots of herbs and vegetables.

"I didn't know there was a little private patio out here." Arkon walked up to the iron fence and rose on his toes to peer over the tall bushes separating the area from the rest of the garden.

"It's only for employees, so consider yourself lucky. I usually come out here to retrieve herbs instead of having to go into the big garden."

She chose a handheld water pitcher and watered the plants.

She could have activated the irrigation system, powered by the sunlight stored in the discs on the top of the roof and the tubes on the fence, but she needed to do something with her hands.

Arkon's presence overwhelmed her, made her nervous. She plucked some dry leaves from the pot of pink cilantro. Her skin tingled, and when she looked up, his stare seemed more intense. She'd almost forgotten why they were out there.

"What did you want to ask me? If you're wondering if I had a chance to visit the ditch, my answer is no."

A wide smile stretched across his face, making him so handsome she wondered if the cosmic gods were having a good day when he was born. It should be illegal for someone to look that good.

"Are you busy tomorrow evening? I'd like to take you out to dinner."

Shock froze her in the spot, and a lump lodged in her throat. Her grip on the pitcher tightened while she struggled for words. Why couldn't she speak? It had been so long since someone asked her on a date. Her brain scattered, leaving her clueless.

What should she say? She wasn't prepared for this. He only met her yesterday. Was that enough time to want to date somebody? Unsure of what to do, she placed the pitcher down and noticed the scar on her arm. At that moment, the scar grew bigger than what it was. It zapped the joy and hope from her. The memory of how it had gotten there dulled the moment, and she retreated back to her corner.

"I'm busy tomorrow." The words came out flat. This wasn't the reply Vanessa wanted to give, but she was afraid of his question about her scar. Eventually, he'd ask again.

What did he see in her, anyway?

"I understand. The restaurant has been busy. Your meat pie is the talk of the village." Arkon moved closer, standing only inches from her. A musky scent seduced her nose, her body.

She shivered, and he noticed. "But I'll be back until you say yes."

Vanessa swallowed. "Why?"

"Why not?" A crooked smile formed on his face. "I like what I see, and it makes logical sense to go after it." His gaze skimmed her face and down her body.

Vanessa, do not melt into the floor.

The copper in his eyes sparked. Was that even possible? She couldn't take her eyes away from his. "I like how I make you nervous, and I especially love how you affect me."

"What do you mean?"

"My body has never reacted to a female the way it reacts to you." He glanced down at his high-tech denim pants.

A large bulge pushed against it. She should have looked away, but she didn't. His reaction gave her power.

"My eyes have never intensified like this. I feel the energy coming from them because of you. Why you? I'm going to find out, Vanessa."

Say it again. Her name sounded precious on his lips. She'd never been precious to anyone but her parents. That was a different kind of affection. The kind he just teased her with was something she'd only dreamed of.

Could she have that?

She saw herself at the center of his eyes. A gold rim glowed around the light amber. Specks of copper glittered in his irises. They looked like gems promising wicked things. Wild things that the previous Vanessa had once loved.

"Can all star-beings do that with their eyes?"

"Maybe." He lifted a shoulder. "But you did this to me. I just reacted." He ran his fingers down her cheek. Not only did she not flinch, she welcomed it. "I had no control over my body's reaction to you. Believe me when I say that I've never reacted this way to anyone in my two hundred and forty-five solar cycles on this planet. This is beyond simple attraction. It's something more, but I won't rush you. Take all the time you need. I'll be around."

He was a lot older than her, but then again, these star-beings had long life spans and didn't look their age. Time was tricky here.

"I'm only twenty-eight," she muttered.

"I know."

How did he know? He probably asked her sister or one of his brothers.

"I'm an investigator for Saedo, so I have my ways of obtaining information."

Was she that obvious to read?

"I've taken up too much of your time today. I should get going. I meant what I said: take all the time you need. But I'll be back. That's a promise. It's an absoluteness. There's no other answer but that, Vanessa."

When he left, a wisp of purple mist lingered and circled in front of her like a secret performance saved just for her. Her hand trembled as she waved her fingers through it. It dispersed, leaving her in awe.

Her heartrate increased because the purple mist greeted her. Arkon's color was purple, and it had come to give her a sign.

Did she believe in fate? It was hard not to. Standing alone outside with the plants and the sky as her audience, she prayed for guidance. If Arkon knew about her past, about her weaknesses and flaws, would he still want her?

Did she have the courage to tell him the truth? Did she want to? Joy and fear collided and left her more confused than she'd ever been.

FOUR

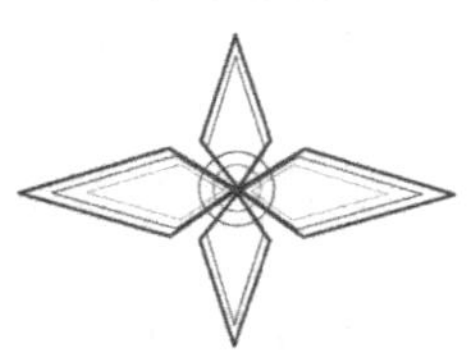

For the next few days, Arkon didn't show up at the restaurant. Disappointment pricked at her. Every time the doorbell chimed, she glanced up, hoping it was him. She even scanned the orders on the virtual screen, but none came in with his name. Every time he didn't show up increased her longing and anticipation. This yearning for him pushed her further out of her cave.

Stop being ridiculous, Vanessa.

This wasn't some high school crush. She was a woman who knew the power of the heart went beyond the surface of physical attraction. Arkon enticed her "wild" side to escape from the dark corner she had found comfort in for so long. She wanted to do all these depraved things with him.

Being near him sparked her imagination in untamed ways. She sucked in a breath at the provocative images of what he could do to her. Her body shivered as she envisioned him kissing her. Arkon brought on an alluring set of sexual nerves that delighted her instead of the stomach cramps, zapping her with electricity. Somehow, thinking of Arkon made her forget the uncomfortable nerves. Was he the distraction she needed? Was he the remedy for her healing?

Travis had shamed this creative side of her, and because of Arkon, she wanted to step out of that cave. Her heart soared at that revelation. It was one step closer to healing herself. And if things didn't work out between them—even though nothing had really started yet—she was thankful that he opened that door for her.

Would he appreciate her wildness? Or would he disgrace her? Regardless, Vanessa vowed to never let a man humiliate, degrade, or dishonor her ever again. She made this pledge the day she left Travis, filed for divorce, signed up at the shooting range, and attended therapy, which she no longer needed. Cooking became her therapy. The creative possibilities were endless, and that abundance allowed her the freedom to do whatever she wanted. Cooking became the temple that saved her.

Arkon ignited an internal storm in her that illuminated what she had been missing all these years. The past few days of longing had pushed her former self further out of hiding. Desire and the need to explore lured her out of the cave.

The more she became her true self, the less the nerves tumbled in her stomach. Were these nerves an internal storm that warned of what was to come? Or were they foreshadowing the clearing of the old? Wasn't that the purpose of a storm? To clean and clear out the old energy? Things that were stuck that no longer served her? Didn't the sun shine with calm weather after a powerful rainstorm?

Vanessa shook her head. She'd been analyzing too much. Arkon would appreciate that.

Damn it, where is he?

She checked her smart pendant, but no messages appeared from him. Had it been a dream that he was outside in the private patio having a discussion with her? Did she imagine the stream of purple mist?

Vanessa let out a breath and gave her mind a rest. She focused on her work, which to her surprise wasn't busy like the previous days. She glanced outside, and the dark clouds loomed in the sky, signifying a rainstorm. This would be her first storm in Saedo.

Abba emerged from the back room. "Business is slow today. I need to get home to help my mother. She's not feeling well and the kids are driving her crazy. I'm going to send Bashlin home and deactivate D-1 and D-2. Klori can stay to help you—unless you want to go home early?"

"I'll be fine. If business doesn't pick up in another hour or two, I'll let Klori go home too. I'll lock up myself."

"Keep an eye on the storm and close early if you have to. I don't want you getting stuck out here. Send me a message when you leave."

She'd driven in a rainstorm before, but not in Saedo. It couldn't be that different, but she didn't want Abba to worry. "I will."

Thirty minutes later, not a single customer came through the system.

"It's dead today." Klori checked her bracelet and pulled up a screen of the weather forecast. "Looks like a lot of rain and wind approaching."

"You can go home. I'll be right behind you. I'll do one walk-through and lock everything up."

"You sure you don't want me to stay?"

"I'll be fine. I'm just going to wait for the Launderjet to finish and then I'll head out. We need clean tablecloths and towels this week."

After Klori left, Vanessa locked the door and went downstairs to check on the Launderjet, which was an innovative washer and dryer using solar light to clean. It also had a section for folding. She took the finished pile of folded tablecloths and divided them up. She tucked half into a drawer and took the other half upstairs.

Something hissed or whispered in the basement. She glanced around but didn't see anything. It was hard to tell with the folding noises from the Launderjet.

She took one step toward the staircase, and her equilibrium wavered. She gripped the railing to stabilize herself. Was it dehydration? Dizziness often occurred when she didn't drink enough liquid during the day.

Vanessa inhaled a breath, found her balance, and strode back upstairs. She placed the tablecloths inside a closet. Then something crashed into the front of the store, shattering glass everywhere. She ducked below the counter to avoid the flying glass shards. The wind howled, and for a moment, it sounded like eerie words. It must have been her imagination because the wind didn't talk. Outside, lighting slashed like blue blades across the sky.

Holy shit.

Could she make it to her personal rider and drive it home? She received her answer when a tree uprooted and flew across the street. Panic rose in her. She couldn't get home. The only thing she could do was stay put until the storm died.

She sent Abba a message but wasn't sure if the message would go through with this massive storm. When she last checked on the forecast, no one mentioned this danger. Was this a hurricane? A tornado?

"Vanessa! Are you in there?"

Her heart leaped when her name cut through the howling wind. She gripped the counter and peered over. Arkon rushed through the opening of the broken glass. "Vanessa!"

"I'm here." She barreled into him.

His arms tightened around her. "We can't be up here. We

need to take cover in case the roof flies off. Is there a basement here?"

She nodded, gripped his hand, and led him down the stairs. He locked the door, followed her down the steps, and surveyed the basement.

"What are you looking for?" Vanessa asked.

"Are there any windows or a door to the outside?"

Vanessa brought him to door that led up to the garden. A small window by the side was covered by a fallen tree. Arkon tugged at the door, testing its security.

"What kind of storm is this? I checked the forecast earlier, and it didn't appear urgent."

Arkon gripped her shoulder, turned her around, and examined her. "Are you okay?"

"I think so. Just spooked."

"This is an unusual storm. We haven't experienced anything like it before."

The unsettling nerves returned. "What do you mean?"

"The clouds we saw on the radar didn't signify a dangerous storm. But what came was different... Engineered."

"What?" Vanessa's mind spiraled at the insane possibility. "Is that possible? Like, could someone actually create a storm on purpose?"

"With the right equipment, I don't see why not. It's all energy. You mix the energies together and you either get something harmonious or destruction. Our experts are looking into it right now." He moved some boxes aside, making a pathway to the couch against the wall. Then he pulled her down to sit beside him.

Vanessa jumped when a loud noise crashed upstairs. Arkon wrapped an arm around her. His hand rubbed her arm, chasing the chill away.

Her heart sank, knowing Happy Belly was being destroyed

and there was nothing she could do about it. "Abba's going to be crushed. This place is her soul."

"I know. But she can rebuild it. Right now, the most important thing is that she's safe with her family."

Did Abba get home safely? Vanessa didn't even know. She checked her smart pendant, but no reply from Abba came through about her closing up. Vanessa prayed her sisters were safe too. She sent a message to all her siblings, informing them she was all right.

"Are messages going through?"

"Most of the radar is being disrupted. Whatever is causing the storm has infiltrated Saedo's security." He looked at his wristband. "I'm on the government net, which has a stronger connection to the Galacto Net, but even that's spotty."

"Can you let Raeko, Maeson, or Osayik know that I'm okay? I don't want my sisters to worry about me."

"I already did." He smiled. "When the first of the lightning struck, I was with Osayik. I told him I'd swing by the restaurant. No one could have prepared for this, and I assumed you were still working."

A thought occurred to her. "Were you working on something the past few days?"

The corners of his lips tilted up. "Why? Did you miss me?"

"Maybe."

The smile grew bigger. "I missed you more than you know. New data arrived, and I had to go with my team to seal up some of the worm tunnels in the ground. We found a dead squirmur that got stuck trying to reenter the hole. Poisonous secretions damaged the soil where it died. We had to clean that up."

Her image of a worm was probably not what he was describing. Her stomach knotted. "What's a squirmur? It's not a small worm like the ones on Earth?"

"No, these are huge, and they're not native to Saedo. We

don't know how they got here. Who brought them here, and why? These were things I was working on the past few days. I wanted to stop by to see you, but these squirmurs are threatening the land with their poison. I had to help my team. I meant what I said before: I'll give you time. Just don't make me wait too long. I'm not the most patient—"

Vanessa held her fingers to his lips. "Do you hear that?"

The wind howled an angry sound and repeated itself several times.

Arkon's brows furrowed, and his face tensed upon recognition of the words.

This is our land now. You must leave.

FIVE

The wind wailed its angry demands as Vanessa tightened her grip on Arkon's hand.

"Tell me you heard that eerie voice." A chill rushed down her body.

"I did." He removed his hand from hers, pulled up a virtual screen from his wristband, and typed a message. "I need to alert my brothers and Chief Mozar about this discovery."

She yearned for the warmth and comfort of his hand but understood the urgency of the situation. "The wind talks. Is that normal for Saedo?"

"Natural wind doesn't speak, at least to my knowledge. But there's nothing natural about this sudden storm. It's either dark magic or someone created it. My gut tells me the latter."

"Why would someone do that?"

"I don't know, but I'm going to find out." The stern voice carried a promise she respected and believed. "There's going to be a lot of damage. I hope everyone found shelter."

Feeling the need to do something, she asked, "Do you want some coffee or tea? There's a backup Coffeewhizz down here in case the one upstairs breaks down. I can turn it on with the solar crystals." One of the best technologies in Saedo was the solar crystals. They absorbed the sunlight used to charge equipment. Abba had invested in a few large crystals.

"Coffee would be great, thanks." Arkon took a seat at a desk next to the couch and pulled up two large virtual screens from his wristband. "I don't know if my messages will get through to anyone right now, but someone will receive this information eventually. They'll have better visuals from the satellites and start some kind of investigation."

Vanessa turned on the Coffeewhizz and made two cups of coffee. She brought the little white cups over and placed them on the side table near the desk.

"Thank you." Arkon sipped and returned to his screens.

At that moment, the lights dimmed in the basement, and Arkon cursed. "Flekken!"

The power grid around the restaurant was probably damaged and activated the stored solar energy in the basement. She never imagined having to use the emergency lights.

As she sat on the couch with the warm cup of coffee between her hands, Vanessa evaluated the situation. She should be freaking out right now, but a strange calm overcame her. She didn't understand what was happening to her. The sudden nerves and now the sudden calmness. What prompted them?

Needing to do something, she activated the restaurant's second computer with a button on the wall. A screen splashed in front of her. Since she had time, she could finish the new menu brewing in her imagination. Would a menu with meals that symbolized hope, perseverance, and survival attract people? She was drawn to those virtues because they were aspects of her life. A breakfast menu that boosted the customer's mood, a lunch assortment that urged them to keep going, and a dinner menu that ended with contentment in their stomach. There was nothing wrong with a happy gut.

Vanessa wasn't sure how Abba or the others would react to such a strange menu. It was even strange to her. Could she pull it off with just unique names? An inner voice urged her along, and she was beginning to listen to her intuition. As she typed up her ingredients and recipes for her experiments, she got lost in the pleasure of creation. She found strength and hope by doing what she loved. Whenever she felt wounded or anxious, she went inside herself and remembered all those things that gave her joy. From that inner temple, she nurtured her gifts and turned the wounds into strengths. While she worked, she forgot about the storm outside, about the fact that she was hiding in the basement, and about the handsome star-being sitting at a desk a few feet from her.

"What are you working on?" Arkon's voice yanked her back into the moment.

She didn't know why, but embarrassment flushed her cheeks. She quickly swiped to a new screen that showed a list of items she had to restock for the restaurant.

"Nothing important, just helping Abba with the administrative stuff."

Arkon only nodded. He probably knew she wasn't telling the whole truth, but he didn't call her out on it, nor did he press on. She appreciated that more than he knew. With Travis, she had no privacy, even in her own mind. Travis had shoved fear into every corner of her body and soul.

Arkon stood too close to her, and sexual energy sizzled between them. The chill she felt earlier vanished, replaced by a pulsing heat that bounced around the basement. Did he finish his work? Why was he staring at her like that?

"Is something on my face?" Vanessa wiped her cheek.

He smiled and her heart flipped. "There's nothing there except beauty." His fingers skimmed down the side of her cheek, along her jawline, and settled at her chin. "This face has been in my mind for days and nights."

Why couldn't she muster up the words to say something? She didn't even know her lips had parted until he traced his fingers along them. The energy between them throbbed, and she lost track of her senses.

She swore it wasn't her brain that urged her to lick his index finger. He gasped at the shock of her seductive act. Vanessa blinked at what she had done and reveled in that spontaneous thrill. That excitement tore away the shield around herself, and the wild Vanessa broke free.

"That was hot, and I want more of it," he said in a hoarse voice.

"Then kiss me." Vanessa rose from the chair and climbed on him. She *climbed* him like a wild animal gripping for dear life. What the hell was wrong with her? No man had ever provoked her this much. Arkon yanked at her senses, making her heart sing.

With Arkon, she felt free to be herself. Her heart thudded at this liberation that was long overdue.

"I want you," Vanessa whispered.

Arkon smirked. "I'm all yours." He crushed his mouth to hers, and she opened for him. His tongue slid in and met hers. Sensations ricocheted through her body like little zaps of lightning, waking up all her nerve endings.

Heat exploded in her core as his mouth devoured hers. Her brain absconded somewhere. She couldn't think. Emotions and desire battled inside her. Arkon woke up a storm within her, and now she let it roar through her with passion and need. She was the storm, and he was the cause of it.

When he backed her against the wall, the coolness toned down the fire in her blood.

"Oh, the things I want to do to you." Arkon veered back to

look at her. His hand slid under her uniform top and found her breast. Mischief danced on his lips. "Do you like me touching you?"

"Yes..."

"Have you thought of me the past few days?"

"Yes..."

"Did those thoughts involve me seducing you? Touching you here." He teased her nipple through the bra. "And tasting you here." His teeth nipped the crevice of her neck.

"Yes..."

Oh, God. Where was her speech?

"Do you want more of me?"

"More." She sighed. "I can't think. I can't even talk with your hands on me."

His copper eyes beamed. "I love hearing that word from your mouth. 'Yes' and 'more' are words I want to hear from you." The huskiness of his voice aroused her. "I love that I can move you like this. I want you melting from my touch. I want you begging me for more."

He seduced her in the most delicious ways.

She soaked her panties, and no shame washed over her. "I guess this is our date after all."

"The first of many. Hold on tight."

She didn't know what he meant. Her mind was still elsewhere, her back still flush against the wall. He took one of her hands and placed it against the bookshelf beside them. Her other hand gripped his strong shoulder for balance.

When she met his gaze, need sparked in those eyes, and she understood his desire. With one hand, he lifted her shirt and held it up. With the other hand, he unclasped the front hooks of her bra. Her breasts sprung free, and he captured a nipple into his mouth. She cried out with pleasure as he took and took.

She'd never been ravished like this. His mouth tantalized

her, and she couldn't look away. She loved the image of him loving her. She loved the way his mouth claimed and took what he wanted. She'd never felt more alive than in this moment.

Desire whipped through her, and she moaned, "More."

He gave what she asked. Her legs tightened around his waist as bliss coursed through her.

An unexpected wave of dizziness overcame her. She didn't understand it. It was more of an intrusion that cut into the beautiful act between them.

She stiffened, and Arkon drew away, looking at her with concern. "Did I hurt you?"

"No, no not at all." He set her on her feet, and she wobbled. "Something's not right." The nerves that had disappeared resurfaced in her stomach. But now, it was ten times more prominent. So prominent she knew something was about to happen. Her gut warned her.

Vanessa re-clasped her bra and collected herself by straightening her shirt. The floor shifted like water was beneath it, and she gripped Arkon's hand for balance.

He cursed and pulled her away from the spot and pointed to the floor. "Watch out for that."

Vanessa blinked and placed a hand to her forehead. "You see the floor moving too?"

Her dizziness reflected the imbalance of the ground. Was her body trying to give her clues all this time?

Arkon gripped his blaster and moved further away. "I see it." His jaw tightened. "I know what's moving underground." He stretched out a long arm protecting her. "Stay behind me."

"What is it?"

"Squirmurs."

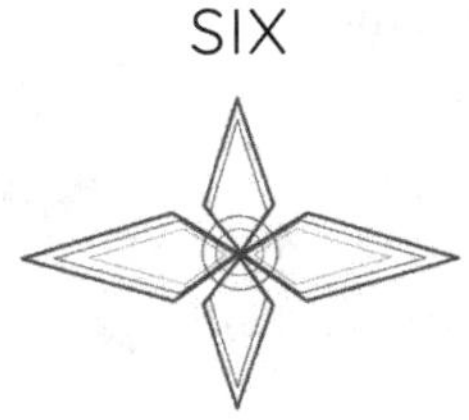

SIX

"The worm monsters that have been digging holes in the ditch? The ones you've been investigating?" Vanessa remembered Arkon mentioning that the squirmurs possessed poison. "Do you think they're infecting Saedo?"

"That's one way to conquer a place: infect it with your own poison, and then heal it after it's yours. It's a cruel way, but Ulkrins aren't loving beings."

"I thought it was my dizziness that made me see strange things." Each time the floor shifted, her stomach lurched. "This may sound weird, but I sense its movement." She recalled her imbalance yesterday. "I felt it yesterday too."

Arkon glanced at her. "We'll need to look into that later. I want to know how you can sense it. If it has some connection to you, then I need to keep you away from it. Keep you safe."

The firm voice and the intention seeped into her heart. No man ever wanted to protect her like that. For the first time in her in life, she felt treasured.

Ten feet away, the floor cracked, and a squirmur's head broke through the cement. Electricity hissed as the squirmur crawled up from the giant hole. It had six antennae around its head. She didn't see any eyes, only thick, segmented skin, which was the only thing that resembled the worms of Earth. It looked more like a giant mutant caterpillar. The monster made a strange sound that chilled her bones. It lurched toward Arkon.

Arkon blasted the squirmur, and the beam sliced a chunk of flesh from the flailing creature. But the injury didn't stop it from jerking toward him. Energy sizzled around its nasty body. Standing so close to it, Vanessa's skin prickled from its energy. Every time energy sparked from its body, a zing zapped her stomach.

A pair of eyes opened under thick skin, and Vanessa gagged in both disgust and surprise. The small eyes glanced around, searching. The bricks from the wall beside her crumbled and thudded to the ground. More squirmurs emerged.

Arkon cursed and yanked out a smaller gun from his jacket. The ball of light at the top of the gun flickered. "Do you know how to use a gun? Just aim and shoot."

Thanks to her dark past, she had experience at the shooting range and learned how to kill a dummy. Though these squirmurs weren't dummies, Vanessa could kill them without qualm. She hoped. She'd find out soon enough. Her hands trembled, but she willed calmness into them.

She grabbed the silver gun from his hand. "I got it."

His eyebrows furrowed with questions. "You can explain how you know what to do with a gun later. Right now, if that thing comes near you, aim and shoot. The gun shoots out energy beams, not bullets."

"Okay."

Another squirmur veered its head from the wall and thudded to the ground. Energy sizzled, illuminating the veins on its body. Again, the eyes on the creature scoured the area in slow motion.

Thunder boomed outside, and the circuitry on the squirmurs' bodies buzzed and radiated in response.

"Did you see that?" Vanessa asked Arkon.

"They're connected to the storm." He cursed and gripped her hand, heading toward the stairs as more squirmurs broke through the floor. Electricity crackled as a separate storm erupted in the basement. "We need to get out of this enclosed space. It's too dangerous."

Arkon shot several blasts at the squirmurs, and they wailed. Rows of sharp teeth glinted from the illumination. The nerves in Vanessa's stomach spiked as more circuitry increased nearby.

As a child, she had a sixth sense for things. She just knew things, felt them as if some invisible guide was beside her. But that ability had stopped when she married Travis and fear took over. Why was her intuition so keen again? She'd contemplate on it later. At the moment, she had to concentrate on staying alive.

Outside, hell greeted her. Dark clouds loomed and sagged, blanketing the area with a heaviness that sucked the life from the area. In the distance, a blue sky peeked through the gloomy contrast. Several squirmurs broke through the ground, angling their heads toward the sky. Arkon blasted a large squirmur that crawled at him from his left. The blasts demolished the squirmur, and its flesh splattered everywhere. One piece slapped against her thigh, and she kicked it off.

Vanessa aimed at one squirmur that busted through the ground twenty feet from where she stood. It opened its mouth as it moved toward her with swiftness. How could this nasty thing move so fast without legs? She aimed and shot out a laser beam into its mouth. It injured the squirmur, but not enough to subdue it. She fired again and again, until she cut the creature clear in two.

She'd never killed anything before. Okay, maybe she had

squashed a few mosquitoes trying to nibble on her, but this was different. When she signed up at the shooting range, her intention had been to protect herself from Travis and anyone who wanted to hurt her. At that time, she needed something to defend, not offend. But ending a life was ending a life, wasn't it? Though guilt gnawed at her, she reminded herself that this animal was a monster. And she had to kill it before it killed her or Arkon. Her action was in self-defense.

More wails erupted, and adrenaline coursed through her as she glanced over at Arkon, who fired at a monstrous squirmur. It wouldn't die. The antennae on its body stood erect as if they were downloading information from somewhere.

The squirmur whipped its body at Arkon, and his back slammed against a large tree trunk.

"Arkon! Are you all right?"

Arkon pushed himself away from the trunk and held up a hand. "Stay over there! Don't come over!"

The wind died down a bit, which was odd since the dark clouds hadn't changed. Vanessa assisted Arkon, firing at the massive squirmur that was twice the size of a tractor trailer. When the creature wailed, lightning shot down into its mouth and energized its body. Its eyes glowed, and Vanessa noticed a device in the space between its eyes.

"Something's going on with the thing's eyes."

Vanessa aimed and fired a beam at its head, but missed when the squirmur crawled out of the way. Did it understand her? Or was someone monitoring them? Monitoring her?

Arkon fired several blasts at the eyes on the massive beast, but it thrashed and the blasts landed on its body. A smaller squirmur popped up from a hole in the ground beside Arkon, and he shot it in the eye. The creature flailed and wailed as energy crackled from its body. A second later, it stopped moving. Not only that, the buzzing energy also died like a switch had been turned off. The darkness in the clouds subsided to a lighter gray. The lightning dimmed, and the thunder weakened.

Vanessa and Arkon exchanged a mutual glance. His expression reflected her suspicion that the squirmurs were somehow related to the storm. Killing them would kill the storm, no doubt.

Standing back-to-back, Vanessa and Arkon fired at the creatures. Vanessa didn't think about anything but destroying these horrendous monsters. It was why she was in Saedo. She dictated how she lived her life. This was her home now, and she would protect it and its citizens. Her new life would not be ruined by these damn worms. The circuitry on the squirmurs dimmed as if something drained them of energy. They took the opportunity and fired more blasts into the creatures.

She never imagined a day where she would hold an actual gun and be part of a real battle. It was beyond storytelling. Her partner in crime was the most stunning star-being, who minutes ago was pleasuring her in the most unforgettable ways. She wasn't finished with him yet. Hope sprouted in her soul because of him, and she wanted an opportunity to see where that seed would take her.

The sky brightened now that the eight squirmurs were dead; four of which had emerged from the restaurant. Two autobuses with flashing lights arrived. As they approached, she recognized the emergency autobuses, which were larger versions of police cruisers, and one fire longship, which was an upgraded fire engine with cutting edge equipment that could easily suppress the fire.

Parts of Happy Belly were ablaze, and Vanessa's heart quaked. Several soldiers jumped out of the autobuses and headed toward them. Dressed in black armor, Raeko and Maeson each gripped a large blaster in their hands.

Arkon signaled to them. "The eyes will kill them faster."

With that direction, Raeko, Maeson, and Arkon fired at the squirmurs beside Arkon.

Osayik hopped out of the fire longship and rushed over to Vanessa. He wore one of her sister's innovative fireproof jackets and pants. It was an idea Inga had come up with after her successful Ingavex collection debut a few weeks ago.

If Vanessa had one of the Ingavex jackets, would that help her kill the squirmurs? But that would require her to touch it, and she preferred killing the nasty things from a distance. Besides, she didn't know how the circuitry on the jacket would react to the circuitry in the worms. Would that create a deadly outcome for her? It was something she would have to tell Inga later.

"Are you okay?" Osayik asked with a blaster in hand.

"Yes. Kill the squirmurs in the eyes. They're creating this storm, or intensifying it."

"Those squirmurs are being controlled by a powerful satellite above the dark clouds. We destroyed it just now. Did you see any difference in the squirmurs?"

Vanessa thought back. "Yes, their circuitry did diminish."

"There's an energy source in this location that's birthing these nasty creatures. There are eggs and poisonous secretions in the soil. We need to eradicate them and clear out the poison. Stay in the longship. It'll be safe there. Call Inga and your other sisters to let them know you're safe."

Her body shuddered from the thought of a womb of eggs under her feet, under the restaurant.

Osayik waved over two soldiers who carried autopumps and activated a driverless fire-hoover. The machine hovered in the air rather than the fire-meanderer that scoured the land searching for victims. She had seen these robotic machines in action on the virtual screen when a fire erupted in one of the buildings near her apartment. They sent in these robots instead of live star-beings to search for any citizens that could have gotten stuck. This kind of invention could save so many fire-fighters on Earth.

Vanessa walked to the longship, but she didn't enter. She leaned against the sleek metal surface and kept her eyes on Arkon. With the blaster still in her hand, she prepared to shoot at any worms within her vicinity. The image of the weapon did something to her. She wasn't the same Vanessa from a year ago. The woman clutching this gun was a fighter, a survivor. She took matters into her own hands now.

Her attention stayed on Arkon as he and his brothers killed the last three squirmurs. Raeko aimed a massive blaster into the worm tunnel and fired out white energy bolts. The ground buzzed, and the zing of energy crawled up her leg. Her body vibrated from the powerful burst. Raeko repeated that action several times, until the squirmurs' wails stopped. He sprayed a blanket of white energy over the soil where the dead worms lay, probably disintegrating the poisonous residue.

The nerves inside Vanessa's stomach subsided as the dark clouds vanished, revealing a blue sky. Her body jerked as an invisible vacuum sucked the negative vibrations from her body. In that moment, Vanessa knew her intuition—the innate knowl-edge—that she could sense these foreign vibrations, both light and dark energies. So far, her body's reaction to everything was a signal that alerted her to trust her gut. When the negative vibrations left her body, it removed blockages from her mind too. This external and internal storm had stirred up a whirlwind of emotions for her. It removed the blockades that had trapped her true identity.

Her sixth sense had been blocked by fear and shame. Now it was back and heightened her intuition to a new level. Her surroundings affected her body. The uncomfortable nerves mimicked the thunderous storm, the calm representing the blue sky—the symbol hidden behind the dark clouds. Most of all, the sexual nerves signified her attraction to Arkon. No wonder she had stomach issues. A cauldron of various energies stirred within her, all wanting her attention.

Could her nightmares about Travis be part of the dark vibrations that left her body just now? Was this her body's way of releasing everything that didn't serve her? Intuition told her yes.

How should she deal with this ability? Which energy should she listen to first? This was a new level of sensory awareness she wasn't accustomed to. Vanessa prayed Grandma Ova could help her.

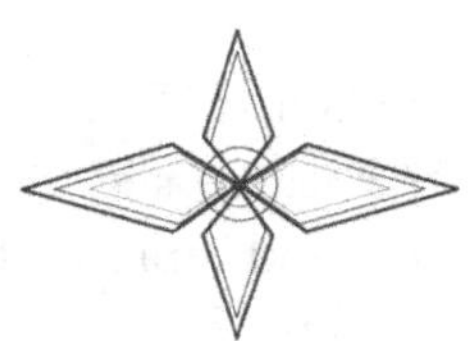

SEVEN

By the time Vanessa entered her apartment, it was around seven in the evening. Arkon stayed with his brothers to assist with the cleanup and discuss a plan to rebuild the area. Sixty percent of Happy Belly was destroyed, including the basement.

Abba was devastated, but she was grateful no one got hurt. She managed to find shelter with her family in their basement, so all was well with her. The Saedo government had a credit reserve to help their citizens. Not only that, the soldiers and any villagers who wanted to help Abba rebuild her restaurant could do so. With everyone's collaboration, Happy Belly could reopen in a month.

Vanessa jumped into the shower and washed off the day's filth. She let the three showerheads beat down on her face and body with warm water. With her eyes closed, images of squirmurs popped into her vision. She flipped her eyes open and shivered. Chills slithered down her body even though she was covered with steamy water.

Who had been watching them through the squirmurs' eyes? And why?

Her temples pounded, and she stopped thinking. She'd

exerted too much energy today. What her body needed was rest and sleep. She stepped out of her shower and plucked a long, fragrant leaf from the citric lotion plant and brushed it along her skin. The citrus smell offered a boost of energy. It reminded her of a clean lemon scent.

Dressed in her soft pajamas, Vanessa sat in her bed thinking. She skipped dinner because she didn't have an appetite. She leaned into her pillow and replayed the events of the day. She thought about Arkon and how he had come for her. So much had changed since that first day they chatted.

Heat bloomed in her center as she imagined the event in the basement before the squirmurs interrupted. She only wanted pleasant thoughts right before bed. Especially, when she needed to sleep. Nightmares would keep her awake, and she couldn't have that. Their kiss ignited a desire in her, welcoming the wild Vanessa to come forth and stake her claim. This was the Vanessa who believed in love and that anything was possible. One man had ripped that belief from her and used violence to threaten her life, keeping her in darkness. Now another man had reached out to her, offering her the freedom to be herself again.

Vanessa didn't even realize she was crying until a teardrop dripped onto her buzzing pendant. She collected herself before activating the video on the call from Sasha.

"Hey. You okay? Emma, Inga, Rita, Isabella, and Nina are all at my place. That was some wild storm out there. Do you want to come over?"

A girl's night out sounded lovely, but not tonight. "Other than extreme exhaustion, I'm okay. I'm about to fall asleep. How's everyone doing?"

"We're good. No one's hurt. Given the extent of the storm, I'm surprised there weren't more casualties."

She hadn't checked the village media. Her chest tightened, wondering about the aftermath. "How many casualties?"

"Maeson said only one star-being died, but he was already ill. Another star-being went after his pet and the strong gale swept him against a building. He's recovering now. Despite the danger, it seems like Saedo was blessed."

It could've have been a lot worse. Her stomach churned as if agreeing with her. When she used to read books on esoteric and new age stuff, she remembered that the mind was linked to the stomach. In college, her studies on eastern traditions stated that what happened in the mind was connected to the gut energetically, which was why when she was stressed, she got indigestion or heartburn, and her stomach inflated for no reason. Knowing this didn't really help decipher her current situation, but it allowed her a different perspective. There were various ways of looking at things.

Her stomach reacted to energy, and it was her job to filter through what was important at the moment.

"Maybe Saedo is blessed," Vanessa said. "We've witnessed a lot of magical things here. It wouldn't surprise me."

"There are a lot of damages to homes and businesses, but those can be replaced. You sure you don't want to come over and hang with your sisters?"

"Thanks, but after today's craziness, I just want to sleep. I'm going to check in on Abba tomorrow. Happy Belly will be closed for at least a month or so."

"I heard. I'm so sorry. Maeson and his brothers will be helping her rebuild. You rest up, and we'll chat soon."

Sasha blew her a kiss and disconnected.

For now, Vanessa was jobless. She didn't mind. She needed the time to learn about herself and this heightened ability. Her mind wandered back to Arkon. She had sensed his energy when he stood on the private patio. She didn't forget the purple mist that wrapped around her. If Saedo lore was true, then she was meant to be with him.

Arkon didn't know she saw his mist. Did it matter? She was attracted to him before she even saw the mist. But she didn't reveal anything because she was embarrassed about how she had reacted when he wanted to pluck the dried leaf from her hair, and she was cautious around handsome men who made her *want*.

She had wanted Travis back then. That desire blinded her and led her down a dark path. She had every right to be careful, every right to protect herself now. She traced the scar on her arm. Unlike before, she looked at the wound and felt no shame. This revelation intrigued her, and she had Arkon to thank for it. He had inspired her to see herself in a new light.

Her pendant buzzed again. She smiled when Arkon's face popped on the screen.

"Sorry, took me a while to get everything done. I wanted to contact you earlier. I was worried about you. Are you okay?"

"I'm fine. Getting ready for bed, actually. How are you doing? Are you home?"

He paused a moment, scrubbing a hand over his face. "I'm actually just outside your apartment."

"You are? Why?" *What a stupid question, Vanessa.*

He smiled. "I was worried and wanted to check on you. See if you needed anything. Is it okay if I come in?"

"Absolutely."

Vanessa clicked off and went to open the door for him. She thought *she* was exhausted. His worn eyes, slouched posture, and the bloodstains on his clothing made him look like he'd come back from war. Well, he did survive a dangerous battle.

"You don't look okay. Do you need something to eat, drink? How can I help you?"

"Can I shower here? I don't think I'll make it back to my

place. I have extra clothes that I always keep in my sports rider when I'm working. Sometimes an investigation can take you down a dirty path." He lifted a duffle bag and showed her.

"Of course. It's this way." She led him to her bathroom and offered him a fresh towel.

While he showered, Vanessa made some tea and warmed up Grandma Ova's herbal soup. Despite his exhaustion, he still worried about her enough to come and check on her. Warmth blossomed inside her.

Arkon strode out to the kitchen wearing a loose top and knit pants. They didn't look like sleepwear, but they weren't work attire either. The casual clothing brought on a different handsomeness. With his work shirt and high-tech denim, he always looked professional, ready for business. But this green man standing in her kitchen with his messy, towel-dried hair which wasn't tied back into a tail, looked approachable and sexy as hell.

He grinned when she didn't stop staring at him. "Like what you see?"

The previous Vanessa would have made some lame excuse or not replied at all. But she was now peeking out from her dark cave to explore. This adventurous Vanessa pursed her lips and said, "There's nothing wrong with admiring a beautiful man. It's like how I appreciate an enticing entrée when it's placed before me."

He strode up to where she sat on a stool at the kitchen island. "Oh, really? What kind of entrée am I, Vanessa?" His eyes darkened, displaying no signs of fatigue whatsoever.

She scanned his face. "That must have been some shower. You don't look exhausted anymore."

"You didn't answer my question. That was a lovely shower because I thought of you when I was lathering myself with your soap and shampoo." He leaned in and sniffed her neck. "I

have your scent on me. I want to know what kind of entrée
I am."

How did the evening change so quickly? Just moments ago,
she was about to pass out. And now, she wanted to nibble him.
What the hell was wrong with her? Arkon could invigorate her
body the way no man had done before. He aroused her simply
by looking at her.

She hadn't been with a man in a while, and this gorgeous
star-being was testing her limits. The intensity in his eyes
revealed he wanted her too. God help them. Sexual tension
swirled in her apartment, and she prayed they could both rest
tonight so they would have enough energy to tackle tomorrow's
agenda.

She twisted her lips. "You're the kind of entrée that I won't
share. The kind that's decadent, hypnotizing, irresistible..."

His eyes glittered with satisfaction as he inched closer and
tipped up her chin. "Orgasmic." A wide grin stretched across his
face. "That's what you were thinking. You were just too embarrassed to say it."

What was she going to do about him? He read her mind,
read her body like they were his own.

"There's something different about you. I'm not sure what it
is." He brushed her cheek with his knuckle. "Something
untamed. Something mysterious. I love it. It's driving me crazy."

"It's a secret recipe. You can find out another time. You've
had a rough day today, and I did—"

His lips were on hers, tasting and teasing. "I need a sample
now." He took his time with the kiss, and she melted into him.
Her back leaned against the kitchen island while his hard chest
pressed against hers. She was deliciously trapped, with no
desire to escape. He nudged her mouth open with his tongue.
Upon contact with hers, he growled, deepening the kiss.

Her fingers dug into his shoulder, wanting more. But she

knew where they'd end up if she didn't stop now. She pressed a gentle hand to his chest and broke off the kiss.

"You captivate me like no other, Vanessa." He ran a thumb over her bottom lip.

"You enchant me like no other, Arkon."

He laughed. "If I didn't have a full day tomorrow where my brain is needed, then I'd have you right here on this kitchen island all night long." His expression turned serious. "I've never wanted anyone like this. What did you do to me?"

What did you *do to* me? But she couldn't muster the words. The more they chatted, the more the sexual tension increased.

She didn't speak, so he continued, "We have things to discuss. I want to know everything about you. I want to know how you learned how to shoot with my gun."

Her past came flooding back, but she didn't flinch. In fact, a calmness accompanied her. "Tomorrow, we'll talk." She reached for the bowl of herbal soup. "Eat this. It'll warm your stomach for tonight."

"Thank you." He considered her a moment before saying, "I'll sleep on the couch. It's wide and long enough for me. If I share your bed with you, we won't be sleeping tonight at all. And you look tired." He scooped up a spoonful and fed it to her. "I don't think you've eaten either. Open up. We can share this bowl of soup and then call it a night."

She eyed him at the unexpected gesture. Her lips opened before her brain even registered what she was doing. No man had ever fed her food, and she found the gesture extremely sexy.

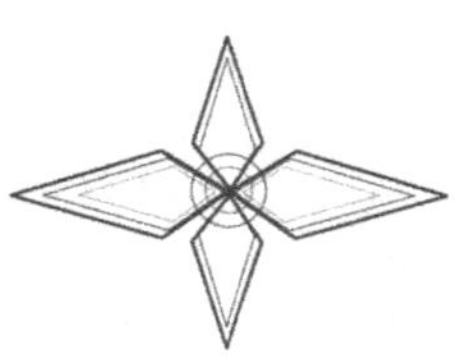

<h1 style="text-align:center">EIGHT</h1>

Vanessa woke to a note on her nightstand. *Urgent meeting. We'll discuss your "secret" recipe tonight. See you soon.*

She blinked, sat up, and read the note again. What time did he leave for work? The time on her nightstand clock showed it was only six in the morning. She glanced out the bedroom window, and the two suns peeked above the horizon like egg yolks, one red and one orange. She stared at the beauty of it for a moment. The daily routine of waking up and getting ready didn't allow for introspection. She was living on another planet with her sisters and star-beings, who, months ago, hadn't existed in her mind.

Of all the places Vanessa could be, fate had placed her in Saedo. Was it a simple act of destiny, or was something else at work here? Did it matter? Overanalyzing was one of her problems, but didn't every woman do that? Sometimes it helped, but most times it complicated the matter even more.

For instance, last night, she enjoyed her flirtatious conversation with Arkon. She loved how he watched her lips take in the spoonful of soup. The way his chest rose and fell, trying to calm his breathing, revealed how much he wanted her. What were his previous mates like? Why wasn't he with anyone? More importantly, what kind of relationship did Vanessa want with him?

The thought of that kindled her heart. A committed relationship hadn't crossed her mind. But here she was thinking about it, *wanting* it, with Arkon. Did he want the same? Or was he only interested in something temporary? There was no doubt he wanted to sleep with her. She wanted the same, but physical intimacy often led to complicated things. Intimacy provoked attachment, commitment, and the desire for more. Was she ready for all that?

Stop thinking too much. You're going to give yourself a headache.

She listened to her inner voice. It knew her best and steered her back to reality. No point in driving herself crazy. She had a busy day ahead of her and needed her brain to function properly.

Despite that, she showered herself with joyful thoughts. The flirtatious conversation between them was something she relished. Where did she even come up with the idea for some damn "secret" recipe? She supposed she could invent something. An idea sparked in her and aroused her at the same time. Damn him.

Arkon lit the torch to her creativity, and now he was going to be its recipient. She wondered what she could do to disrupt his organized ways. His mind understood numbers and charts. What would happen if she introduced something that was the complete opposite of that? Would that intrigue or irritate him?

Before she could focus on her idea, she needed answers and guidance from Grandma Ova on a different matter. Danger lurked in Saedo, and if she could help keep her new home safe, she'd do it.

"I wondered when you'd stop by to see me." Grandma Ova gestured for Vanessa to sit down on a white chair next to her. On a round table was a plate of pastries topped with floral petals, two mugs, and a pitcher filled with green liquid.

The back deck faced a flourishing herbal garden with fragrant flowers. A sweet scent snuck up her nose, and a small bird that resembled a goldfinch with six wings fluttered over to the table. It chirped a lovely song that made the flowers sway back and forth. Or was that her imagination? She didn't sense any strong breeze that could shift the herbal plants in this rhythmic way.

"Are the herbs reacting to the birdsong?"

Grandma Ova smiled and made chirping noises that drew the bird closer. She dropped a few seeds onto the table for the adorable yellow bird. "My plants love when these little felicitees grace them with their soothing melodies. With their six wings, they spread joy everywhere." She poured the green liquid into the mug and offered it to Vanessa. "This is a good way to start your day. It's a blend of my green lantern fruits and some healing herbs." She jerked her chin to a tree with purple leaves and green fruits dangling from it like lanterns.

Vanessa sipped the drink, and the sweet and sour taste reminded her of apple juice. She grabbed a fruit tart from the tray, bit in, and fell into heaven. "Oh, these are divine. What's in it? I could eat a dozen of these."

Grandma Ova chuckled. "The fillings are made from my calmberries." She pointed to a bowl with triangle-shaped purple berries. "They're not too sweet. They help calm and balance your nerves, help your body maintain equilibrium. When our bodies are out of balance, discomfort occurs."

The topic of nerves wasn't a coincidence. "Did you sense

something from me when we were at Sasha's house the other day?"

Grandma Ova tucked a lock of white hair behind her ears. The classic hairdo suited her face and was the result of Sasha's skilled handiwork. That reminded Vanessa, she needed a trim soon. The red mane was getting too long, too wild.

"I sensed your frequency that day. It was powerful, but I also knew you had no idea what was happening. I couldn't pry." She stared out at her garden. "There are certain things in life that need to be left to their own accord. I knew you'd come here. How? Intuition. Just like how you had a hunch to seek me out."

Vanessa nodded. "The nerves started about a couple of weeks ago. But they're stronger now. I sense all kinds of energies. Why am I feeling them now?"

Grandma Ova's eyes warmed. "First off, I want you to know there's nothing wrong with you. What you have is a gift from the divine. You've always had it, but it was dormant. Something kept it hidden, but it's waking up and nothing can hold it back now. You're ready to hone that skill."

"How do I know which feeling to listen to when I feel so many at the same time?"

"Experience. You learn to trust your gut. We all have this ability. Some are more in tune with it. I can't tell you how to read your emotions or senses. Your body, your gut will let you know." She patted her stomach. "Your stomach is very important. Your entire body is its own system. Some of us forget that. Your body will let you know the difference between a negative and positive energy, what is urgent and what is nonurgent. Energy can't really lie. It can mask itself for a while, but that gets tiring, and the true energy will eventually seep through. Your body will be able to read that. It'll take practice. Don't rush it."

Maybe her mom wasn't making things up about her great-

great-grandmother being a priestess. Maybe Vanessa inherited her gift.

"I've been sensing those squirmurs for the past two weeks. My stomach kept acting up, and I didn't know why."

"Those damn worms. I pray the soldiers will destroy every one of them."

"Why are they here? What's their purpose?"

Grandma's cheerful face turned somber. "They want to infect Saedo soil. Our province is blessed with fertile soil that can grow all kinds of vegetation. The energy in Saedo is exceptional."

"I think the squirmurs were doing more than just infecting the soil. Their eyes connected to the lightning in the sky."

"I have no doubt the Ulkrins are part of this. They've wanted this territory for too long. They need to be eradicated." Grandma Ova got up from her chair. "Come with me. I want to do a little experiment." She took Vanessa around the house to an area with more trees and bushes.

They approached a tree that had curly branches and blue leaves with orange veins. The shape of the leaf wasn't abnormal. It was almond-shaped, about four inches long. A hissing sound came from around her. She turned, looking for a bug or some animal.

"It's the tree." Grandma Ova pointed to a low branch hanging near Vanessa. "Touch it and see what happens."

What kind of test was this? Vanessa hesitated and furrowed her eyebrows. Suspicion rose in her, even though Grandma Ova had no reason to harm her.

Vanessa placed her hand on the veiny blue leaf. It hissed upon contact, and electricity beamed on its veins. "Shit!" She pulled her fingers away, fearing she'd get zapped. "What's going on?"

Grandma Ova smiled and reached for a leaf. Nothing

reacted with her contact. She plucked the leaf off the tree and twirled it around. "I was right. You have the counterpart of its frequency. There are polarities within everything. Male to female, light to dark, hot to cold. They are polarities."

Her conversation with Arkon about polarities flashed in her mind. *We exhibit energies that complement each other.*

Vanessa thought she knew some of what was going on with her body, but now?

"I don't understand at all."

"This tree. You have a frequency that resonates with it, therefore it reacted. You have its polarity. That's also a gift."

"Why me? I'm just a chef. I love to cook interesting dishes. What am I going to do with that gift of knowing and sensing?"

"Don't undervalue yourself, Vanessa. We all have a part to play in the Cosmos. It doesn't matter what your occupation is. What matters is in here." She tapped her chest. "Your corra. What's more important is how you use that gift. Will you use it to help or hurt someone?"

Vanessa twisted her lips, still trying to wrap her mind around the whole idea. Grandma Ova dropped the leaf into Vanessa's palm. "Get to know it. I'm certain it would love to know you. If you have any questions, I'm here. Or you can always call me."

The leaf warmed her hand, and the veins continued to illuminate. She pulled the small notebook out of her purse and placed it between two pages. Inside the notebook was a collection of ideas for recipes. She kept the book handy for when she needed to jot down ideas. She could pull up a virtual screen from her smart pendant, but there were some things she preferred the traditional way. She liked pen to paper.

Vanessa had one more thing to inquire before she went home. "I saw Arkon's purple mist. I didn't tell him yet."

Grandma Ova clasped her palms together, and her eyes beamed. "Oh, this is lovely to hear! It's a blessing, Vanessa."

"What if it doesn't work out?" Insecurity snuck in, but she couldn't help it.

Grandma Ova sighed. "You didn't tell Arkon because you wanted to see if he feels the same way without the purple mist swaying his emotions?"

It felt like a privilege to stand next to someone so wise.

"You know everything, don't you?" Vanessa smiled. She wanted to talk to someone about the purple mist. Someone who knew about its history. If she told her siblings, they'd tease her about it and wouldn't stop hounding her with questions.

"It comes with living a long time."

"I'm attracted to him," Vanessa said. "But I also want to be careful. I don't want to make... a mistake."

Grandma Ova embraced her. "As long as you listen to your corra, you won't. Your past is in your past. Use that lesson for this present moment." She brushed a hand down Vanessa's hair like a grandmother would do to her grandchild.

The gesture comforted Vanessa more than she thought. "Thank you for everything."

"You're welcome. Now, get going. I sense you have something exciting planned tonight?"

Heat flushed on Vanessa's cheeks. "I'm not sure what you're referring to."

Grandma Ova angled her head. "I remember those days. Don't be shy. Have fun. Show him the fearless you. Introduce him to things that are outside of 'numbers and charts.'"

Vanessa grinned. "I guess everyone knows him well."

"He needs a female who can show him a different way of evaluating and investigating. Drag him outside the box. Do it with finesse and he'll go willingly."

Grandma Ova wiggled her eyebrows.

Vanessa's shoulders shook from laughter. Sexual talk with someone who was older than her great-great-grandmother was more interesting than she could ever imagine. "I can't believe we're having this conversation."

Grandma Ova waved a hand. "There's nothing wrong with our conversation. We're two women having an intelligent discussion on sexual energy, which is a form of creative energy." She winked.

"Thank you for entertaining me." A thought popped into Vanessa's mind. "Maybe you could help me with this idea..."

When she shared it with Grandma Ova, the woman burst with laughter. "I thought I was innovative, but you? I love that creative mind of yours. Let's go inside. I'll show you how to make it work."

NINE

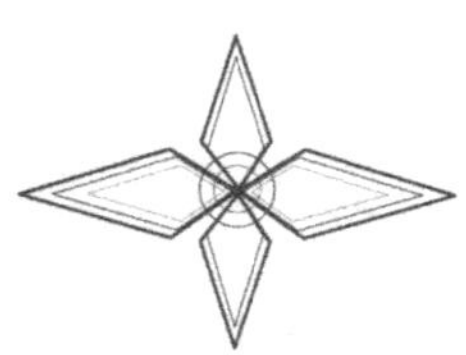

After spending another hour with Grandma Ova, Vanessa's mind sparked with a plethora of ideas. Not only did she have something exciting planned for Arkon, the menu she had been trying to create for her very own line of foods and snacks formed in her mind. Once she settled on the details for the innovative menu, she'd propose a collaboration with Abba. If Abba refused, then Vanessa would look for a venue to start her own restaurant. Excitement filled her, and she knew she was on the right track.

Grandma Ova's unique character added an amusing layer to Vanessa's day. She encouraged Vanessa to release any limiting beliefs that she wasn't good enough. Somehow, the wise star-being knew and lured the stories out of Vanessa. Vanessa shared her past and her intentions about Arkon.

Grandma Ova showed Vanessa her other gardens. The farming techniques opened Vanessa's mind to new possibilities she had never considered. If Earth had this mindset, then the human race could live longer and healthier lives. The star-beings in Saedo possessed ideas that enhanced their land, made it magical. Was this why other star races wanted to conquer them? Steal their treasured land? Why didn't those star races administer the same or similar methods to their own regions? She supposed that answer came down to the fact that it was easier to take over something already established than to start anew.

Lazy bastards.

She didn't want to waste any more energy on that thought. With enthusiasm, Vanessa rushed into her apartment with a bag of plants Grandma Ova prepared for her. Ideas on how to seduce Arkon pecked at her, each one wanting her attention. She dumped the plants onto her kitchen island and sorted them out.

She recalled the meal he ordered at the restaurant and concluded a man like him wanted meat. He had tried the Nelson meat pie along with a side salad. The old adage was that the best way to someone's heart was through the stomach.

On one hand, it might seem like she was indifferent to the fact that she had just fought squirmurs yesterday and the threat was still prominent. On the other hand, she didn't want fear looming over her head and stopping her from living. What was wrong with a little adventure to make the best of the moment? Absolutely nothing.

She pulled out her little notebook of recipes and set it aside in case she needed a reference. She didn't think so. What she planned was clear in her head.

She separated the herbs and vegetables she'd be using and replanted the others in her little indoor garden by the window. A chef needed all her ingredients handy when inspiration struck. From the pile on the counter, she grabbed a plant called hematiss. It had oval-shaped leaves with purple edges. The plant produced peapods that reminded her of soybeans, the difference being the purple color. Apparently, this hematiss plant imitated the flavor of blood in meat, including the texture. It could elevate her vegan dishes even more, and it also meant that fewer animals needed to die. She imagined what humans on Earth would think about this marvelous plant that also balanced the hemoglobin in the body. Vanessa thanked Grandma Ova for the short science lesson.

Tonight, Vanessa was going to experiment to her heart's desire. For the next few hours, she busied herself with chopping, blending, and searing a hematiss steak that mimicked the one on Earth. She tasted a sample and moaned.

"I like that sound coming from you."

Vanessa jumped at the voice inside her apartment. She whipped her head to Arkon, who leaned against the wall that separated the living room from the kitchen. His eyes glinted with curiosity while his thick arms crossed over his chest, studying her. He wore a white button-up shirt with the sleeves pushed up past his elbows and high-tech denim. Why did that casual outfit make him so seductive?

How long had he been standing there? "How did you get in? I didn't hear the doorbell. I didn't feel my pendant buzz either."

"The door wasn't locked."

She blew out a breath. "Must have forgotten to lock it when I rushed in." Her excitement to cook had blurred logic.

He stood beside her, and heat increased. "Why were you rushing?"

What should she say? *Oh, I'm just chopping up ideas on how to make you moan out my name.* Or *I'm creating something that'll make you ravish me.*

She decided to keep the surprise from him. "I was excited to cook you a meal." That was the truth.

"Oh really?" He peered over at the kitchen table where she had bowls and plates set up. "Whatever you're making smells delicious. When I came in and saw you immersed in your own world, I didn't want to interrupt you. I love watching you work. And now that I know you're making something for me, that's an extra treat." He rested a hand on her lower back. "It deserves a reward." His hand lowered and squeezed a butt cheek. "I couldn't wait to get out of my meeting to come see you. I've been thinking about you all day."

Desire pooled at her core. She placed the energetic knife down, fearing she might lose a finger with this sexual energy building between them. She swallowed, hoping to moisten her throat.

Arkon noticed and traced a finger along the throbbing vein on her neck. "I like how I make you lose focus."

She looked into those darkened eyes. "I'll be the one who makes you lose your concentration. Your sense of organization will scatter for me. *Because* of me."

Amusement flashed in his eyes as he considered her. "You've been scheming, haven't you? So calculating. I normally like knowing the solution ahead of time, but this intrigues the hell out of me. What do you have planned for me, beautiful?" He brushed away the hair that fell over her forehead. "Your hair is like you. So much fire, so much heat." His fingers tangled in her hair. "It drives me crazy."

Her heart thudded as intense energy swirled around them. A stream of purple mist emerged from behind him and snaked around her waist. She didn't point it out, and he didn't say anything. He was probably used to seeing his own mist color.

The mist ribboned around her, kissing the skin on her arm and hand. "You started the fire, and now you'll have to pay for it." She reveled in this freedom to tease without fear of repercussions, without the dreading that a man would put his hands on her.

"Why did it take so long for us to meet?" he asked.

She didn't have a chance to answer. His mouth covered hers, kissing her with desperation. "I can't wait for later. I want you now." He lifted her off her feet, placing her on the marble island. The stone cooled her inflamed body. He nudged her legs open and stood between them. His hand slid under the hem of her dress, moved up to her thigh, and cupped her breast. "I'm hungry. Let's cook something now." A mischievous smile slanted in a way that promised delicious things.

"Are you playing chef?" She challenged him, and the green of his skin darkened a shade. How come she didn't notice that before? "Your skin changes color?"

"Only when I'm exceptionally aroused. If I'm the chef, then that makes you my main course."

In seconds, her dress was on the floor, leaving her with only a sheer black lingerie set she had worn specifically for this evening. The bra barely covered her breasts, and the diamond-shape of the panties locked his eyes to that area. She bought this set a week ago to support Inga's new lingerie collection made from edible fabrics. The one she chose had a provocative flavor with an extra surprise.

His hands cupped her breasts, and she arched toward his touch. "You're so perfect." He had amazing hands with amazing thumbs that did amazing things to her. Her brain melted, and she blamed that for her repetitive words.

She wanted to see all of him. She tore off his shirt, and a button bounced off the wall. Did she really do that? This wildness in her had been repressed for too long. An eyebrow arched, and his gaze followed the button as it clinked to the floor and rolled somewhere.

He faced her with amusement in his eyes. "You're so ferocious. It's shocking and I love it."

Vanessa smiled at the adjective no one had ever used to describe her before. She had a ferocity to live up to now. She yanked the leather strap from his hair. The messy mane of brown hair fell just past his chin and framed his angular face perfectly.

The green of his skin fluctuated, and his brown eyes glowed copper, revealing the need coursing through him. The same desire scorched through her, but she wanted this moment to examine him, like a chef understanding her ingredients before she started her masterpiece. Her fingers traced the strong lines on his broad shoulders and caressed the curve of his bulging biceps. Her fingers traveled to the thick pectoral muscles and slid down to his firm abdomen. Each movement was a claim to a territory that now belonged to her. He was hers.

How could anyone be this impeccable? Her hand remained on his rock hard abs as she pondered using it as a chopping board to mince herbs.

"Your touch is tearing me apart," he said in a husky voice. He gripped her hips, pulling her closer.

Vanessa wrapped her legs around his waist like a snake ready to jump her target. He clamped his mouth over hers, and his tongue swept in and sent a jolt straight to her core. His playful tongue tantalized hers. The muscles in her loins tightened as an internal tornado spun her in a dizzying storm of pleasure. She couldn't think, couldn't breathe.

Arkon intensified the kiss as she clawed his shoulders and back, digging her nails into his flesh. Need coiled inside her as she wanted more. Subtlety did not exist at the moment. He offered feistiness, and she gave it right back. She moaned out a pleasure that she didn't recognize. Was that a purr from her?

He tasted like a savory blend of spices, so musky, so male. His scent of cedarwood with a hint of nutmeg tossed her into another whirlwind that rocked her body.

"I can't get enough of you." He lowered her to the counter, his mouth skimming the column of her neck.

Fire followed his every touch. She slipped into another world, and the room blurred, leaving only her and the raging need that begged for more. This was the intimacy she craved, the kind that hadn't been accessible to her until now. This green man worshipped her like she was some damn goddess. She quivered when his hand found her wet center, and his mouth claimed a nipple through the sheer edible bra.

At the taste, he lifted his head. "Sinful cocktail flavor? I'll take damnation if that means I can have you. I'm going to devour every inch of this bra."

He feasted on her breasts, one after the other, eating away the thin layer of fabric laced with an intoxicating blend of cocktails. As he savored, lights hissed and sparkled from the contact of lips to material. He let out a sound like a satisfied animal. The innovative construction of this bra deserved an applause, especially when Arkon growled, "More."

True to his words, he licked every inch of the edible cuppings. She watched him savor her, and a bolt of need slashed through her. She loved how his mouth mapped around her breasts, over and under. Her body responded to every kiss, lick, and bite, hips bucking against the bulge of him.

"You have no idea what you're doing to me. I'm burning inside." The copper in his eyes reflected her fire.

Her heart hammered knowing she lit the spark in him. She entered the wildfire storm with him, not fearing if she got scorched. Vanessa heard fabric rustle and the clank of his belt dropping to the floor. On her elbows, she studied the magnificence of him, gasping at his size. The glorious length of his manhood beckoned her.

Arkon leaned over, lowering her back onto the marble island. "I'm not done with my entrée yet." He spread her legs and palmed her tiny diamond-shape underwear that clung to her skin like magic. "What flavor is this?"

She couldn't find her voice to answer. When his mouth pressed into her secret place, she cried out his name and writhed from the onslaught of pleasure.

"Decadent chocolate. My kind of dessert." His hands lifted her buttocks, ravishing her like she was his meal.

Waves of pleasure whipped her from side to side. She gripped his hair, holding on as the tornado tore through her, rippling down her spine. "Arkon..."

A shuffle of clothes sounded as he retrieved the Safe-Sex Spray and covered himself. Curiosity had her reaching for his bulge. An interesting texture coated the surface. "This adds a unique sensation when I'm inside you."

Their eyes met, and he slipped into her. A moan escaped him as he dove deeper and deeper. The texture added a new layer of sensitivity that sent pleasure skyrocketing through her. She loved connecting with him this way. She sat up and wrapped her arms around his neck, dragging his mouth to hers. They moved in rhythm as he continued to thrust into her. Each thrust broke a barrier until all that was left was her bare soul and the truth of her heart.

At that acknowledgment, purple mist encircled them. The mist knew what was best for her before she did. Now, she confessed it to be true. Now, she *felt* its power.

His body tensed, and his heart hammered. Feeling powerful, she intensified the kiss and pushed him further into his own monsoon. With a forceful thrust, he bellowed her name, and she'd never heard anything more delightful. His body convulsed as she wrapped her arms around him, embracing him. The tender gesture surprised even her. She clung to this sensation that overwhelmed her heart. Love glittered like stars, and she couldn't avoid it.

His strong arms cradled her as his chin rested on her head. "That was some course. The best recipe for an out-of-this world con-*coc*-tion." His manhood throbbed at the statement.

Laughter burst from her. "You have a dirty mind." When was the last time she had so much fun with a man?

"I'm like most males. I'm just honest about it." He pulled out of her, the contraceptive spray dissolving on his length. A sly smile curved on his lips. "But I think *your* mind is more creative than mine. I bet it's *messier* and *dirtier*. I see it in your eyes. Show me."

Arkon saw her true self, and that perception deserved a reward. Vanessa pushed her recipe notebook aside and reached for her bag. She dug out a container, picking out a translucent blue petal that reminded her of a rose. The petals were infused with the midori melon drink that Grandma Ova helped Vanessa mix. Grandma Ova had a trellis of these blue melons.

Still naked and baring everything to her, he eyed the petals. "What are those?"

"Something that's going to inspire you to look at things differently." She slid down from the kitchen island and held out a petal that had a massaging property. "You had your turn. Now it's *my* main course."

She gripped the length of him and placed one delicate petal over him. It wrapped and tightened around him like a second skin.

His breath hitched, and he let out a delightful curse. "Flekken! What are you doing to me?"

She smirked and pulled out the stool, nudging him down. He leaned into the back of the stool, watching her every move. He trembled as she placed the other five petals onto his length. His breathing increased, and lust filled his eyes.

On her knees, Vanessa gripped him. "It's going to massage and tingle and end with a cooling sensation."

"Flekken."

She displayed her creative skills and proved that her spontaneous culinary invention would be a bestselling novelty item.

TEN

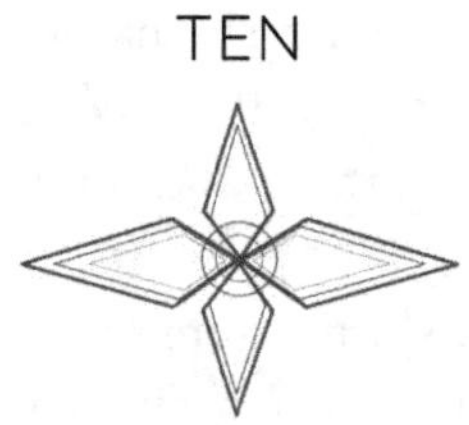

Hours later, Vanessa curled up on the couch with Arkon, fully clothed.

A smile beamed on his face. "You invented those... things? They're genius."

Pride swelled in her chest. "I did. You inspired me to explore my creativity. It doesn't have a name yet. I'm thinking once I save up enough credits, I can open my own restaurant, my own food boutique."

He looked at her. "Is that your dream?" He took her hand in his, and his gaze landed on the scar on her arm.

"Yes. I stopped dreaming after..." Her body stiffened. Was she ready to tell him?

"After?"

She inhaled a gulp of air and prepared to bare everything to him.

Arkon stared at the scar, and his thumb caressed the wound as if his movement could wipe it from her. "Did it have anything to do with this mark?"

Vanessa nodded. "Unfortunately, yes. For the longest time, I pushed my dreams aside. I had to work on myself first before I could go after those dreams again."

"No one has the power to take away your dreams. No one." His voice carried a lethal edge she hadn't seen in him. His eyes steeled. "Who needs to die for this? What's his name? Where is he? I can get a spaceship there and do what I need to do in no time."

His protectiveness shifted something in her. No man had ever wanted to protect her this way. "Don't waste your energy on him. I've put it all behind me. He's my ex-husband, and he's in prison for a long time. I wasn't the only one he abused."

Though his voice was calm, its thunder rippled through her. "What did he do to you? I want to know everything."

Arkon listened as Vanessa spilled the darkness from her past. "It all started with the verbal abuse when I didn't deliver dinner on his favorite plate with his favorite drink. The name calling wasn't enough for him, so he got physical. I remember the first time my lips bled from his attack. I was shocked and confused. How could someone who claimed to love me, hate me so much?"

Arkon's face tensed. Vanessa placed a gentle hand on his cheek, letting him know the horror no longer bothered her. The story flowed out of her like a river traveling toward the ocean and dumping all the unnecessary things at the delta to start anew. Arkon was her ocean, her new beginning. Revelation dawned on her. She was no longer haunted by Travis, her dark past because she found something brighter. She found Arkon.

With that thought in her heart, Vanessa continued. "I didn't want to believe that the abuse was really happening to me. Shame and guilt overwhelmed me. I thought everything was my fault. I turned to cooking as my salvation. It was something I loved before I met and married him, so I knew I was good at it. The process of making something from my heart saved me and kept me sane. I had hoped that he'd change one day. It wasn't until he took my favorite knife—the one I used to cook his dinner—and threatened me and my siblings that something snapped in me. It was as if that blade cut away the mental chord he had around me. I called the police, left him that day, and warned my siblings of his threats just in case he'd follow through on them. I filed for divorce. Then I signed up for the shooting range because I feared he'd come after me. I killed a little fear each time I shot into that dummy. After a while, I got good at it."

Arkon didn't interrupt and gave her enough time and space. When she finished, he released a heavy sigh, and his jaw clenched.

"I could kill him for what he did to you. There's no excuse for that kind of behavior."

"He's slowly dying behind bars. He's claustrophobic, so the punishment is fitting. He's suffering."

Arkon pinched the space between his brows. "I can live with that for now."

His concern for her brought back the wish she had tossed out into the Universe that fateful night. *I deserve a man who loves me regardless of my wounds.* Could Arkon be him?

Vanessa's heart thudded at that thought. Deep inside her, she knew. But did he feel the same way about her? She wasn't referring to the obvious physical attraction. Did he love her the way she loved him?

Her body shivered from that admission. There was no shame in loving someone, even if the person might not love you back. Could she deal with that? She wasn't sure, and she was afraid to ask. At this moment, her vulnerability was too high. She couldn't withstand that kind of blow to her heart, so Vanessa kept that emotion to herself for now.

"You know my darkest secret, but I don't know yours. I have

questions," Vanessa said. "What's your dream? Your worst fear?"

The question softened his expression. "I have a younger sister, Ameeya. My parents died in a spaceship accident a while ago. My dream is just starting to form now. Before that, I didn't have one." He looked at her. "But my fear is losing my corra."

He didn't answer her question, but she let it pass. She focused on other aspects of his response. No parents and a fear of losing his heart showed they shared some similarities. "I feel like I have so much to learn from you."

He flashed a wide smile. "I'm willing to teach you anything you want. In and out of bed." His eyes twinkled with mischief.

Purple mist emerged and floated around them. She waved a hand through the purple ribbons. "I've never seen purple mist until Saedo."

He flicked her a glance. "You see it too? You see my mist color?" The somber expression twisted her stomach. "When did you first see it?"

"When we were on the private patio."

"Do you know its significance? Why didn't you tell me sooner?"

"I heard about it, but I wasn't sure if it was true." Why did she feel like she did something wrong? "I didn't tell you because I didn't think it mattered. It's Saedo lore that could be true, or not."

The distrust in his eyes stabbed her heart. The indignation on his face and the muscle twitch on his jaw revealed someone who wouldn't listen to reason right now. Why was he angry at something so trivial? She realized she didn't know his past. Did he have monsters that gripped him the way hers did?

Nerves churned her stomach. The unease brought her mind back to the squirmurs. How was Saedo going to destroy these monsters?

Arkon's wristband buzzed, and he pulled up a video screen displaying Raeko. "Can you meet us at Derwood Creek? The radar just picked up a squirmur nest. We need to eradicate it."

Arkon got up from the couch, heading toward the door. "Why didn't we catch this earlier?"

"I don't know. Something's masking it from the radar. I'm rounding up as many soldiers as possible. The Guards of Finntoro will meet us at the border. They don't want any squirmurs invading their land. Make sure you have your armor. It could get ugly."

Vanessa's chest constricted from Raeko's words.

"I'll be there as soon as I can. I have my uniform in my rider. I'll change when I get there." Arkon disconnected and faced Vanessa with concern. "I have to go now. We'll talk when I return. Don't go out."

With that, he left her apartment, leaving her confused and crushed.

ELEVEN

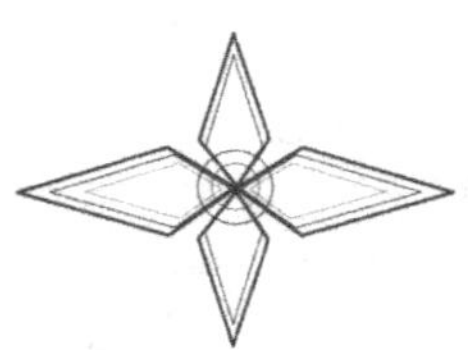

What exactly just happened between them? Why was he offended that she didn't tell him about the purple mist? Was that detail so important to him? What did she miss?

Sadness and disappointment washed over her, making her feel exposed. Feeling cold, she wrapped her arms around herself, protecting something she didn't know. She didn't see her relationship with Arkon lasting. Their communication was off. It was better to step back before things got more serious.

But things were already serious. She was already in love with him. It happened faster than she wanted. The heart worked in strange ways that she couldn't control. The icy way Arkon looked at her knifed her in the chest. The distrust and the disgust in his eyes pushed her away.

No man had the power to make her feel little again. She had been truthful all along, and if Arkon didn't see that, then he wasn't worth it. He didn't deserve her.

The more she thought about it, the angrier she grew. Anger cramped her stomach, like someone was twisting her intestines into knots. The unexpected pain grabbed her attention. Something awful was about to happen.

A hissing sound echoed in her apartment. With a hand to her stomach, she tried to locate the sound. It came from the notebook. She flipped it open to the blazing blue leaf Grandma Ova had gifted her. The veins on the leaf brightened to an electric blue. The leaf rose from the page and floated in front of her. Vanessa didn't sense any fear from it. If anything, its presence soothed the ache in her stomach. The buzzing of the leaf calmed her nerves.

How did she know that? She just did.

Her heart leaped when the leaf swayed back and forth as if a breeze was inside her apartment. It suspended itself in front of her face, and the leaf morphed into a single eye, greeting her.

"Holy shit." Instincts pushed her back a few steps from the floating eye. Was it real?

Logic told her to run from the freaky image, but something else held her in place. Again, Vanessa didn't sense fear, and the eye wasn't bloody or gory. Power radiated from it, asking her not to fear. Her mind understood the request.

She chose to listen to it.

An ancient wisdom entered her mind. The eye blinked, floated closer to where she stood, and images formed within the eye that created a little portal she could look into. Colors and abstract images jumbled together.

Don't fear us. We're here to help. You have energy that resonates with us, and that makes you important. He needs your help. Saedo needs your help.

A sincere truth rang with those words and settled in Vanessa's stomach. Within her stomach was a battle between nerves that shouted something was wrong and gentle nerves that calmed her. She reminded herself that these sensations were merely guiding her, making her aware of her environment.

The eye-leaf expanded like a movie screen. It showed Arkon fighting off squirmurs larger than the ones they fought earlier. A red squirmur with a bright beam on its forehead monitored on the side. Was this a snapshot of the future? Arkon wore the same outfit he had when he left her apartment minutes ago. He was all by himself. Where were his brothers? Why weren't they helping him?

Dark clouds emerged from the squirmurs, creating a storm around Arkon.

He needs you. Go to him.

Though her stomach twisted in knots, the calming energy enabled her to decide with a clear head.

First, she sent Arkon a message. "Are you okay? Where are you?"

While she waited for a reply, she retrieved the blaster he gave her the other day and changed into high-tech knit pants and a long-sleeve top. The dress she wore wouldn't help in battle. She never considered herself a fighter, but here she was, fighting for a man who changed her life.

No reply came from Arkon. Maybe he was too busy fighting off the squirmurs.

Vanessa didn't know if the eye-leaf could understand, but she asked anyway. "How can I help?"

You'll know what to do. Trust your intuition. The eye of the storm will show you.

One thing she learned with all this "magical" wisdom was that nothing was ever clear. Messages lay between the gray areas, the "this and that." Perhaps they didn't want to toy with her free will. If they told her exactly what to do, would that change the outcome? If they let her choose, then she made her decision all on her own.

Arkon needed her, and that truth surged in her heart. No matter what had happened between them, she loved him. There was nothing wrong with loving someone. If anything, Arkon inspired her to stand strong and acknowledge the survivor she was. She no longer feared her past. She reclaimed her dreams, and she reveled in the fact that she could explore her creativity in ways she never imagined. Arkon opened that door for her when he opened her heart.

Vanessa didn't have time to contemplate. The energy from the eye burst in her apartment, pulsing against her body as a portal opened. Not knowing where the portal would take her, Vanessa stepped forward. With Arkon's safety prominent in her mind, she entered the storm, figuratively and literally.

TWELVE

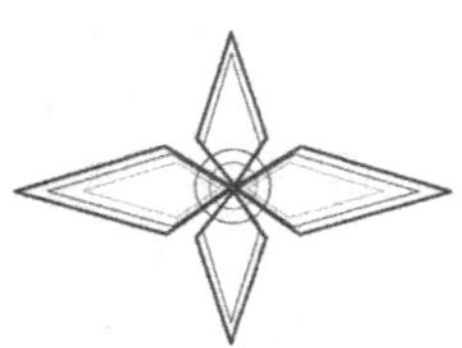

Inside the portal, total darkness and silence enveloped her, nudging her forward toward the gathering of twinkles that beckoned her. Intuition told her this silence was the space between worlds, between the inexplicable scopes of time.

As Vanessa approached the twinkles, the wind howled, and lightning slashed. *This is our land now. You must leave.* The words boomed louder than when she heard it the first time in the basement.

The tunnel of light splashed a screen that showed the danger before her. A squirmur leaped at Arkon, while another whipped its segmented body at him. He fell to the ground.

"Arkon!"

Vanessa fled through the portal, and the opening closed behind her. The blue leaf hung in the air, sizzling with energy. She gripped it, and the energy seeped into her skin, into her blood, into the marrow of her being. Her body shuddered and buzzed.

What the hell? Vanessa had questions, but she didn't have time to waste. She tucked the leaf into the front pocket of her pants and clutched the blaster tucked in the back of her waistband. She aimed the blaster at the squirmur and fired. Through the thunder and wind, Arkon didn't notice or hear her until the squirmur wailed from her blast.

Arkon whipped his attention to her and rushed over. "Vanessa! What are you doing here? How did you get here?"

Genuine concern flashed in his eyes instead of the distrust from earlier.

"I came to rescue you." *Like how you rescued me and my sisters.*

Despite the danger surrounding them, he smiled. "Be careful. These squirmurs aren't like the ones we battled. These are stronger, smarter."

The wind howled again like someone was blasting the words through the speakers.

On cue, the squirmurs thrashed their bodies and electricity glowed through their skin. Arkon fired at them, but only sent the electricity sparkling. Thunder lit up the sky, and that was when she saw his rider smashed against the tree. The broken road looked like an earthquake had occurred.

Ten squirmurs surrounded them, buzzing with electricity that matched the brilliant blue lightning in the sky. The red one, the one who had been eyeing them from the side, wailed a command. In that moment, Vanessa's body hissed.

Arkon gawked at her, and worry wedged in his forehead. "Are you okay?"

She glanced at her body, and electricity coursed through her, flashing like the squirmurs. The only difference was that hers was purple. Heat warmed her, but not in an uncomfortable way. In fact, confidence and power surged through her veins. Intuition kicked into gear, and she knew what to do.

As the squirmurs approached, Arkon stepped in front of her, protecting her. That simple movement confirmed he still cared for her, and whatever happened today, they'd resolve their personal issues.

She reached for him, but stopped, fearing her touch might electrocute him. A squirmur cried out as it twisted its fat body toward him. Vanessa moved around Arkon, and punched the worm right in the eyes. Her circuitry blasted into the squirmur's body. The force of the contact threw her away from the squirmur and she fell on her butt. Arkon ran over and assisted her up. Purple energy took over the electric blue of the worm. The worm exploded, and the spying device embedded behind its eyes flew out and thudded near Vanessa's foot.

"They're flekken watching us! I'm going to kill those damn Ulkrins!" Arkon blasted the device, and a loud hissing erupted in the sky.

The red squirmur cried out, and the bloody beam on its forehead brightened. A laser aimed at Arkon's chest, and a second one landed on her chest. Fear crippled her, and Arkon reached for her hand. A surge of purple mist grew from his body and hers. The squirmurs moved toward them, but the mist spun around and kept them at bay. Thunder roared and the wind increased, howling and whipping things around. A cyclone of twigs, leaves, rocks, and other debris spiraled around them.

The purple mist increased in size and density, taking over the cyclone that trapped them. The mist became its own storm, spinning and spinning. As it spun, it pushed the debris away, keeping Vanessa and Arkon at the center of the storm. The mist moved of its own volition. The wind and the lightning didn't affect it.

Something urged Vanessa to reach out and connect to the purple vapors. On contact, the purple electricity from her body joined the mist and illuminated the entire area. The red squirmur retreated from the burst of purple energy. It cried out as if calling for help. The squirmur's storm increased, lightning enlarged, and thunder screamed louder. Despite the chaos, Vanessa sensed a calmness.

You'll know what to do. Trust your intuition. The eye of the storm will show you.

The voice from the eye-leaf echoed in her head. Arkon blasted a squirmur that broke through the soil near her foot. She gripped his hand and squeezed. "We need to kill the red squirmur with our fused energies."

He didn't object; he didn't ask any questions. He just nodded, giving her his trust.

Vanessa wasn't sure what she was doing. All she knew was that she had to listen to this inner voice guiding her.

She reached into her pants pocket and pulled out the blue leaf. Energy sizzled from it. She held it out and looked at Arkon. "Together."

Both held an end part of the leaf, and purple energy vibrated from it, rippling out to the vicinity. Purple lightning with vapors surrounding it shot up into the sky and broke the squirmur's storm apart. They shifted her body toward the red squirmur that was crawling away, and with their intentions, a purple bolt of lightning lashed into the creature. Red flesh splattered everywhere. A device clanked by her foot.

Arkon kicked it aside. "We can dissect that for information."

Still holding onto the leaf, they each turned in different directions and targeted the various squirmurs. Their intentions sent blades of power toward the creatures. When they had obliterated all the squirmurs, they aimed the leaf toward the sky. A powerful spear with purple mist shot straight up. A thunderous explosion erupted in the sky. Another explosion followed elsewhere, then another like a domino effect. The explosions went on for another minute.

Vanessa turned to Arkon. "What's happening?"

"We just destroyed whatever brought the storm. The

Ulkrins are working with another star race to create a device that could send storms to other regions. Saedo is a treasured land. We have great resources, and they want Saedo. They won't stop until we stop them."

Vanessa glanced up at the night sky that was now cloudless with the moon glowing brightly. She picked the device up from the red squirmur and offered it to Arkon. "What happened on your way to your brothers?"

"The squirmurs blocked my path." His wristband buzzed.

Raeko appeared on the screen. "You okay? What happened? We were all worried."

While Arkon explained to his brothers, Vanessa glanced at the leaf in her palm. "Thank you for your guidance."

Thank you for listening, and thank you for trusting yourself. We'll see you soon.

Vanessa tucked the leaf back into her pocket, and Arkon came up beside her. "The emergency crew will be here soon to clean up and retrieve the device. We'll hitch a ride home. Is it okay if I spend the night at your place? We have some things to discuss."

She reached up and wiped the blood smear from his face. She didn't want any squirmur residue marring his handsome face. He clasped her hand and placed it over his heart.

A smile bloomed on his face. "Thank you for coming to my rescue. I didn't expect that at all. I wanted you safe at home, where nothing could harm you. And here you are, fighting beside me with a blaster and a blue leaf. No female has ever done that for me."

Vanessa didn't know what to say. She handed the blaster back to him.

"No, you keep it. You handled yourself well with it. All those classes you took paid off."

They sure did.

"That leaf is exceptional, and I want to hear all about it." Regret swam in his eyes. "I'm sorry for my behavior earlier. There are some things you don't know about me, and it's time that you do. After you hear what I have to say and decide to walk away from this relationship, I'll understand."

That idea suffocated her. What was he going to tell her? Was this a good time to let him know she loved him? Was there a good time for that kind of confession?

If he was going to her tell her something that broke her, then she should bare her heart now. A shattered heart had nothing to share.

"The leaf showed me you were in trouble, and I came because... because I've fallen for you." She met his eyes. "Despite what occurred between us, or what may happen later, you've opened my heart—my corra—in a way no man has done before."

He tipped her chin up. "Are you telling me you love me?"

Vanessa lifted a shoulder. "It sounds like it."

"I love the sound of that." He pulled her in for an embrace. "I feel the same. I know the emotion is still new between us, but it's so strong I can't ignore it. But just because it's new and hasn't had time to develop appropriately, doesn't mean it's not real. I've realized that things don't follow a linear pattern, and that no organization, no charts, could ever determine a specific outcome. I've learned to accept the idea that it's okay to not follow a straight line."

"Are you telling me I've inspired you to think outside the box?"

He smirked. "It sounds like it." He ran a thumb across her cheek. "All I ask is for you to keep an open mind about what I have to say."

He had no idea how wide her mind had opened.

THIRTEEN

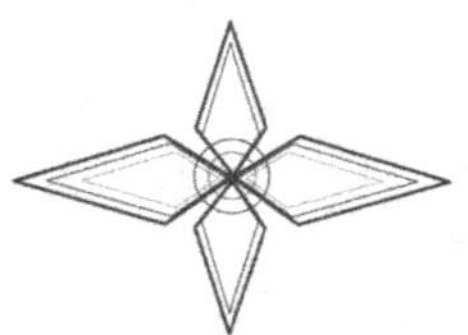

Vanessa woke up early the next day and made breakfast. She created her version of vegan sausages, meat cakes from the hematiss plant, and fruit pancakes. Arkon was still sleeping in her bedroom. When they got home last night, both of them were exhausted. After a shower together to wash away the filth of squirmurs, they passed out in her bed.

It had been a while since she last had a man in her bed. She loved waking up with Arkon's warmth. His presence felt right. Purple mist continued to swirl around her apartment, and she was getting used to it. She tucked the blue leaf in a special box by her bedside. Its energy had subsided, and that told her the threat was eliminated for now. The erratic nerves that had gnawed at her stomach also disappeared.

Thinking back, her body had been giving her signs about the danger all along. Though she didn't know exactly what it was, the discomfort was a signal to be extra cautious, to be aware of her surroundings, and to notice little symbols. Like her intuition, her body was giving her clues in its own way. She embraced her ability now and promised to practice more. Perhaps one day, she could communicate with the eye-leaf and even the mist. One important thing she learned in Saedo was that possibilities and magic were endless.

She steered her attention back to the task at hand and went to her indoor garden to cut some chives. A purple bloom had appeared between all the herbs. Or rather, the herbs appeared like protectors to the flower. This flower signified her union with her starmate. A blessium grew in her garden, but hers had two opened purple petals that appeared like two hands offering up something or receiving something.

Did that image mean anything? Probably, but she didn't have the brain power to dissect the symbolism.

"Well, hello there." Vanessa studied the flower. "It's good to see you."

Arkon wrapped an around her waist. "Are you talking to your plants again?"

Too focused on the flower, she didn't hear him walk up. His hair was tied back with the leather strap, and he smelled of her citrusy toothpaste.

"I'm talking to a flower. A purple flower that looks like it's breathing out purple mist."

Arkon stared at it and looked at her. "I guess the Saedo lore is true. We're starmates. We're meant to be together." With a hand on each shoulder, he swiveled her toward him. "Together, we're stronger. Just like last night, we destroyed those heinous creatures as a team."

The flower sighed and caught their attention. The purple mist emerged from the flower and formed an abstract shape. "It's a face."

"Looks more like an eye to me." Arkon angled his face, trying to gauge what shape the vapors made.

"Maybe it's both, part of the same thing." She stared up at him. "I want to research Saedo lore. I think we need to gather all the information to fight the Ulkrins. We stopped the squirmurs this time. But what else are they planning? We need to be prepared."

Arkon veered back and smiled. "You're right, and I love that you care for Saedo. Chief Mozar and my brothers are working out a plan. The Guards of Finntoro helped my brothers destroy the squirmurs' nest last night. Apparently, the Ulkrins stationed an energetic cloud around that area that masked the nest from our radar. Maybe their fake cloud malfunctioned and that allowed our radar to pick up the traces. It's hard to tell because we obliterated all of their energetic clouds and satellites last night from the explosion. Raeko mentioned he felt the soil ripple with energy."

"Did he ask you questions about it?"

"I gave him a brief explanation. I was too tired. He can get the long story from you if he wants to." He led her to the kitchen table and sniffed at the breakfast she made for him. "I could wake up every morning like this. We can discuss that after I tell you what I didn't get to say last night." He nudged her down on the seat and scooted his chair closer to her.

"Are you ready to share it? If you're not ready, I can wait. I'm not going anywhere."

"I've been ready, and I've been waiting for the perfect time to tell you. But then you surprised me about the purple mist, and I overreacted." He reached for her hand. "I used to have a mate. She told me she saw my mist, and I believed her. I didn't have any reason not to. We were together for five solar cycles. She inspired me to step out of my comfort zone. Do spontaneous things that didn't have an absolute answer. Then one day, she wanted to end things, telling me that she was in love with someone else. She confessed she never saw my purple mist. She knew about the lore connecting starmates, and everyone understood they were rare, so she created a lie to get it. I was too blinded by love to think otherwise."

Vanessa's heart ached for him. "I'm sorry to hear that. Love makes you do strange things, and I don't say that to excuse her actions. But love has its lessons for all of us, including me. I was blinded by love too. But none of that was my fault. If we're genuine in our feelings, then it's never our fault."

"I was afraid to step out of my comfort zone again when I met you. But my feelings for you were too powerful to ignore. I had no choice. Being with you taught me that possibilities are endless, and yes, there could be more than one answer to things."

Vanessa beamed with pride. "I'm learning that an absolute answer isn't so bad either. It depends on perspective. We're an absolute couple, and nothing can change that. One plus one is two. Me and you, forever."

"How did I end up with such a wise woman?" The copper in his eyes brightened, and she saw her reflection in them. "When you told me you saw my mist, the betrayal from the past resurfaced and punched me in the gut. The pain came back and I couldn't think clearly. I was falling for you too fast, and I couldn't understand it. Questions bombarded me. Were you telling me the truth? Why didn't you tell me sooner? What were you trying to achieve? A storm of emotions whipped inside me at the moment, and I needed space to think things through before I could talk to you."

Vanessa squeezed his hand. "I'm not like her. I didn't lie to you. I would never do that. Communication is important to me, it's the one thing that will make or break a relationship. I value what we share with each other." She looked him in the eye. "I didn't tell you because I was afraid. I was afraid you'd want me *because* of the lore. I wanted to be sure that you were attracted to me regardless of fate. I wanted to know you cared for me because you wanted to."

Arkon pursed his lips, thinking. "You didn't want the lore to influence my decision to be with you."

"Exactly."

"I respect that." He lifted her hand, flipped it over, and kissed her palm. "Remember you asked me what my dream was? I didn't give you a direct answer because I didn't want to frighten you. My dream is to be with you, to make a life with you." His hand rubbed the scar on her arm. "I love everything about you, from your scars, to your mind, to your creativity, and to your dirty culinary aspirations. Everything." His smile stretched for miles. "That novelty is going to be a bestseller. I just know it. I volunteer to be your test subject, your only test subject."

She laughed even as tears rolled down her cheek. Her wish to the Universe echoed in her mind. *I deserve a man who loves me regardless of my wounds.* She closed her eyes and acknowledged her appreciation. *Thank you.*

Arkon offered her a tissue. "I have an idea that could make us great business partners. I'm good with numbers, and you're fabulous with your culinary creativity. In fact, you're the most effective and dangerous chef I know." He leaned in closer. "You could essentially kill me with an overdose of pleasure, and I'd go willingly."

Smiling, Vanessa pushed him away. "I see what's *really* on your mind."

"I'm serious about the partnership. Your dream is to open your own restaurant. My dream is to be with you and make you happy. I have the credits for it. We can open it together."

The idea intrigued her, and she appreciated his support, but what if her restaurant failed? She didn't want him to invest in something that could end up being unsuccessful. "I don't want to take your hard-earned credits. I can save up. I mean, what if it doesn't work out?"

"You mean us or the business?"

"Both."

"Business is risky, and so is love. There's nothing wrong with investing in someone I love. Don't deny me that. This passion to help you is the one thing I'm absolutely sure about."

His words touched a sensitive cord that kept the tears flowing. Why was she so damn sensitive right now?

"Do you need me to make you a chart of the pros and cons? Because I will."

Vanessa took the second tissue from his hand. "How can I refuse this kind of love? I'd be a fool to do so."

"Excellent. After breakfast, we can visit Abba's restaurant. Did you know she decided to sell it? She wants to open a smaller restaurant down the street from her house to be closer to her family, and she doesn't need the current space anymore. Heard it from the property owner. It could be yours if you want that space."

Vanessa placed a hand on her heart. That was the perfect space with the large yard. Not to mention the memory where they met. "I love that space."

"Perfect then. We can take a look and decide on a name."

"How about 'Trust Your Gut?'"

He angled his head in consideration. "It's you—it's perfect."

Joy filled every part of her body. She had a man who loved and supported her. She never imagined finding him on another planet. But the Universe had its own plans, and she was grateful for them.

She leaned over the table and kissed him. "Just so you know, you've inspired my special culinary assortment called In the Mood novelties. They'll be special orders for adults only. I'm going to ask Inga to promote them with her edible lingerie collection. I think they'll do well together."

Arkon grinned. "Just so you know, I'm always *in the mood* for you, love. In fact, I'm free after breakfast."

Vanessa almost choked on her herbal drink. "Do you have books on Saedo history? I want to start my research."

"You want the ancient texts. The Village Library has a collection of sacred Saedo texts. We can stop by and ask your sister to make copies for you. The originals can't leave the library."

"Great, I'll contact Rita and let her know we'll swing by."

As the two lovers enjoyed their breakfast and immersed themselves in exciting conversations about their future, they didn't notice another petal opening from the purple flower. Or that a breath of purple mist emerged from it and twined its way through the window on a sacred mission. The mission to wake up the family that would assist in protecting Saedo and all its residents.

Thank you so much for reading! I hope you enjoyed Arkon and Vanessa's story. Read Rita and Jarzell's story in **An Alien Lore.**

Don't miss out on any new releases. Sign up for my newsletter!

http://callazae.com/newsletter/

UNLOCK THE ANGEL
EXCERPT

Blurb

His heart is engulfed with the dark… but for her, it awakens with light.

Disheartened with relationships, Cathy Lu concentrates on her career. But the magic around the August Full Moon lures her to a stunning angel who illuminates her desires in a way that makes her wonder if everything is just an illusion.

As a seraph bound to blood, death, and responsibility, Daedriel has never had a long-term lover. But one kiss from Cathy unlocks everything for him, making him want the forever.

Can he keep her safe while evil swarms around them? Or should he keep her away from him, away from all the darkness that threatens him?

Excerpt

Cathy

Cathy Lu hammered a nail into the plank of wood on her back deck and thought about her ex-boyfriend—specifically his family jewels. How would he feel if she pounded him like this nail? Yes, it was a morbid thought, but as an ex-girlfriend who had been betrayed, she had every right to feel that way. Cheaters deserved a painful punishment, didn't they? They had to feel all the pain they'd bestowed on their significant other. That should be a law. So, she envisioned all the things that made her feel better. Wasn't that part of the healing process?

She pounded another nail into the wood and admired her work. She'd learned a few handy things during her two-year relationship with Gavin. He had promised to renovate her deck and the new studio she was adding to her house. But promises from a cheating man rusted over time. It made her wary of men's promises in general. Now, she depended on herself.

Cathy had kicked Gavin out of her home four months ago when she discovered several text messages and emails he'd been sending to two other women. She should have suspected something was up when he came home later than usual or when he had unexpected phone calls that took him into another room. She had been too trusting.

She considered herself an intelligent woman, but when she discovered the truth about Gavin, it made her feel stupid. Love had a way of distorting things, and she couldn't afford another loss like that. She was careful now. She had to be. Her heart had shattered, and she had hammered it back together. She sighed at the symbolism of hurting Gavin and also piecing herself together by hammering a single nail. Maybe that idea could make its way into her new greeting card collection.

Despite it all, she had moved on, mending herself one step at a time. Time spent alone gave her the retrospection and the clarity to focus on her company, Luminous Press. She had a small team of people who worked for her, making sure her journals, novelty books, greeting cards, and other miscellaneous products were delivered on time to their vendors. She and her mother, Celia, had started the company eight years ago, when she was twenty-five years old. Working with her mom had taught her how to be a successful businesswoman and a decent person who looked at things with compassion.

Be gentle to everyone. You never know what someone is going through. You can't measure someone else's pain from a personal scale.

Everything was different when it was personal, wasn't it? The measuring scale changed when you were the one experiencing the pain. It was all perspective. No one could ever understand that misery until they'd experienced it themselves. Standing on the outside made it difficult to see the storm from within.

Her mother's wise words echoed in her mind. If only her mom were still alive, she'd comfort Cathy, reminding her that not all men were the same.

Victor Perez knocked on the glass panel of her sliding door, opened it, and stepped out to the deck. "I'm all done for the day, Cathy. The two bathrooms, kitchen, and living room are all spotless now." He smiled and removed the apron, folding it into his hand.

Cathy rose to her feet and stretched her back. She appreciated his gesture even though she knew that his wife, Rosa, needed him more. Rosa and Victor had been cleaning Cathy's house for the last two years until she fell sick with a thyroid disorder that had gotten worse in the last few months. They had planned on early retirement, but life threw a curveball at them that readjusted their plans. So now, it was just Victor supporting his family. Their daughter, Lizzi, who was also Cathy's friend, lived in New York. She'd come home to visit and assist them whenever she could.

"Do you need me to help you with anything else before I head home?" Victor asked.

The weight of his wife's illness sagged on his face even with that adorable smile. The eyes and facial features revealed a lot of things that people didn't realize.

Cathy tapped the hammer against her hand. "I've got it handled. Thank you, though. Please send my best to Rosa. How's she doing?"

Victor sighed, and his shoulders drooped. "She's improving slowly. Her hair isn't falling out as much now with the new medication. We have a doctor's appointment next Friday to follow up. I'm praying for good news."

Cathy squeezed his arm. "Please keep me posted. Rosa's a strong woman. I'm sure she'll overcome this."

He nodded, giving her a warm smile. "Thank you."

"You don't have to come next week. I'll see you in two weeks," Cathy said and noticed the worry lines on his forehead. "Don't worry. The payment won't change. I figure you could use that time to be with Rosa. Besides, I live here alone. How much of a mess can I possibly make in a week?" She knew most people hired a cleaning service every two weeks, but she kept Victor and Rosa on once a week. She liked them and didn't mind supporting their business. They had been cleaning for her mom before Cathy hired them for her own house.

His eyes watered. "I don't know what to say."

"Say that you'll make the best of it. Life is short, Victor. Be with your family when you can."

After Victor left, Cathy resumed her work. She tried to take the same advice she gave to others, which was why she planned a three-week vacation to regroup. She hadn't taken a break in a long time, so this vacation was a treat. Her best friend, Sydney, the vice president of Luminous Press, could manage while Cathy was away.

Cathy planned on using this extra time to brainstorm the greeting card collections for the next few seasons. Designing the art for the greeting cards was one of the fun parts of her business. It activated a different area in her brain that wasn't crammed with numbers, profit margins, production, deliveries, and so on.

A bird squawked somewhere, and the unique sound broke through the silence. She rose from the deck and glanced toward the woods that drew her to this place. Beyond the trees was the gorgeous Prudent Lake. She had brought a tent out there a few times and slept under the moon and stars. She was due for another adventure soon, especially with the August Moon Festival next week.

When she was six years old, she looked out her bedroom window at the full moon and saw a gold rim around it. It glowed for a while, mesmerizing her. At that time, she had felt a warmth brush against her face when the rim glowed, but it could've been the imagination of a child believing in magic and fairy-tales. Because of that childhood experience, Cathy felt an odd friendship with it. The moon pulled at her in an inexplicable way.

With nature as her background, Cathy found the stability to move on after her mother's death a year ago. They used to come to Prudent Lake on vacation when she was little, so living here was somehow reliving the precious moments they'd shared together. She had no idea where her father had gone. He left when she was six, and that broke her mother.

Another squawk rang out, and she looked around, trying to see the bird or hawk that was making the lovely sound. She spotted nothing. She went into her kitchen, took out the bag of birdseed, and filled her bird feeder. "Enjoy your snacks."

She loved watching the birds gathered in her backyard like

it was their playground. The enchanting sounds of nature were the spa that relaxed her.

Her phone rang, and Sydney's name flashed on the screen. "Hey, I don't mean to interrupt your vacation, but I just wanted to remind you about the August Moon Festival next Friday in Boston. Are you going?"

The August Moon Festival was a special time of the year for her family and her heritage. In the past, she'd attend the event with her mother. But this year, Cathy wanted to do something personal, something without the crowd. She could celebrate the holiday right in her backyard.

"I'm going to pass. I'll just do something small at home."

"Are you sure?" Disappointment leaked from Sydney's voice. They had met in college and became fast friends.

Cathy appreciated Sydney's intelligence and foresight when it came to business. Outside of business, Sydney was the trusted friend every woman deserved. Without Sydney's support in both business and friendship, Cathy didn't know if Luminous Press would be as successful as it was.

"Yes, I'm not in the mood for crowds this year."

"Hang out with us girls," Sydney said. "We love talking shit about cheaters, and there's *a lot* of them. That means we'll have plenty of conversations and drinks."

Cathy laughed, appreciating her friend. "We'll hang out soon, I promise. I need to hire a contractor to finish my studio. I want to get it done before I return to work. And I'm brainstorming the new greeting card collection too."

"You're *supposed* to be on vacation," Sydney said with a disapproving tone.

"Yes, *Mom*. I know, I know. I don't mind it, though. The creative part is fun for me. You know that."

"I do, and that's why I'm not driving over there and dragging you away. Do you want me to bring you back any mooncakes, lanterns, food, or anything?"

"No, thanks. I already placed an order for the mooncakes. They're being shipped to me. Have fun, and don't forget to make your wish to the Moon Goddess. You never know. She could make your dreams come true."

"I'll be sure to make a long list for her. She should find something on there to give me," Sydney said.

"You are the queen of lists." Cathy could imagine the several pages of demands from Sydney.

"Hopefully, the Moon Goddess won't find me too high-maintenance. I only want intelligent, sexy, humorous, and thoughtful men to come to my door. I'll even settle for their snores and messiness." She let out an unladylike laugh. "Maybe we're doomed, Cathy. Maybe we're meant to be alone, which I don't mind now and then. But sometimes I miss that connection, you know? What happened to all the decent men who wanted gorgeous women with acute intelligence and creativity?"

"We're not doomed," Cathy reassured her best friend. "We're special, and special things are rare. 'Decent' men are rare too. We just have to wait for our turn. In the meantime, live life. Have fun. The right guy will come along. You're a fabulous catch, and you need someone who measures up to you. Don't ever lower your standards to be with someone."

Though Cathy offered words of encouragement to her friend, a part of her wondered if there was a decent man out there waiting for her. After her failed relationship, it was hard to believe in happily ever after.

"This is why Luminous Press is successful," Sydney said. "You always turn the bitter into beauty. We make fabulous journals and greeting cards that give people hope."

"Hope is the lantern that gives off light when you need it."

Cathy didn't know why these deep thoughts were spewing out of her so easily.

"Oh, I just thought of something!" Sydney said with excitement. "What do you think of these for Valentine's Day cards? *Do you want to be my lantern? I burn for you. Let me light you up! Let's illuminate the night together.*" She giggled. "They're cute and cheesy, but I have a weakness for that stuff."

"I think they're perfect." Cathy grinned into the phone, admiring the creativity of her friend. "I'll let you handle the next Valentine's Day Collection."

"Cute and cheesy, here I come."

Their conversation carried on a few more minutes before Sydney had to run to a meeting.

Cathy tucked her phone into the back pocket of her shorts, picked up the hammer from the deck, and dropped it into the pouch of her tool belt strapped around her waist. She strode over to the unfinished addition on the side of her house, which also shared the same deck. With hands on her hips, she envisioned the complete studio that would allow her more space to create.

Another squawk erupted nearby. Cathy glanced over to the tree next to her just in time to see a splash of glistening white feathers disappear into the woods.

What kind of bird was that? She loved discovering strange animals and rushed down the steps in the hope of catching the bird. Hoping it perched somewhere close for her to peek, Cathy made her way into the woods.

About ten feet in, she didn't see anything and headed back to her deck. As she walked, a strange sensation pulled at her. She wobbled a bit and blamed her imbalance on the lunch she missed. She got caught up with all the hammering. She glanced at her phone; it was already six in the evening. It was time for dinner. *Shit.*

She got back onto the deck and was about to enter her home to make a sandwich when she heard the squawk again. This time, it sounded further away, but the call echoed through the woods like gentle music that penetrated through the clutter of your mind, catching your attention. Not only that, she heard a loud swoosh of wings flapping somewhere. A powerful gust of wind carried an interesting scent to her nose. Was it citrus or sage? She wasn't sure, but she liked the aroma. It soothed her.

She waited a beat to see if she could hear it again, but silence reigned. Was it her imagination? Or was there some large bird out there? Perhaps it was someone's exotic pet that had gotten lost.

She'd investigate after she fed herself.

Daedriel

One flap of wings and he soared across the serene skyline, over dense trees and sparkling lakes, taking in the mesmerizing view of Earth. He glided through the air, letting the wind massage his face and feathers.

In a horizontal position and ten feet above the water, Daedriel glanced at his reflection. Dark hair, a cream T-shirt, black leather pants, and iridescent blue wings glistened against the glassy surface of the lake. His blue feathers darkened from the warm colors of the setting sun. One set of wings flapped and allowed him to soak in the fresh air that invigorated his lungs. The other two sets of wings rested in their invisible state. There was no need to exert more energy than necessary. The air on Earth was denser than that of the Celestial Realm, but his body could transmute the air quality to suit his need.

As a seraph from the twelfth-dimensional matrix, Daedriel possessed power more potent than any other angels—even the Archangels, who were his friends. Well, some of them, anyway.

He smirked, knowing that if they heard him, they'd object and challenge him to a duel until all their feathers were destroyed in the battle. But those days of carefree play amongst friends hadn't been around for a long time. He missed it, but there were important priorities now. The battle to protect the Celestial Realm had intensified and thus tossed all the angels into defensive mode. The threat to their home and their existence hung in the balance as darkness multiplied within the Universe.

The Celestial Realm was a sacred place within the twelfth-dimensional matrix that was also a doorway to higher dimensions. Some he had visited, while others remained a mystery to him because to get there required an energy boost he didn't have. What he possessed allowed him to travel up to the fifteenth-dimensional matrix. His responsibility to rein in the darkness kept him busy enough from the twelfth dimension and below.

The darkness continued to infect and distort the Celestial Realm, which was why he was on Earth trying to locate the traitor, Rask. He had once been a trusted guard, but he stole the Reversal Black Tourmaline, a rare gem infused with darkness. A regular black tourmaline crystal absorbed and neutralized negative energy by turning it into nothingness, giving that energy a new beginning. But dark powers had manipulated one black tourmaline eons ago, reversing its natural abilities. The Reversal Black Tourmaline had absorbed and stored so much dark energy that it became a weapon for the dark side. The dark could pull power from that stone to feed itself.

Years ago, the seraphim angels had won it back from the dark. They brought it to the Auric Circle, where powerful celestial forces extracted the darkness to be alchemized slowly, naturally. To destroy such a powerful gem could wreak havoc on all life forms.

Where was Rask? Daedriel had tracked his energy to this place known as the state of New Hampshire in the United States of America. Of all places, why was Rask here on Earth, in a land filled with trees and lakes? Was Daedriel being misguided? That thought crossed his mind several times, but he trusted his instincts. Something here was calling him, and he had to find out what it was.

As he neared the home he'd just bought two weeks ago, his pet parrot, Tika, flew up to greet him.

"You're late." The white parrot squawked with its purple beak, gliding beside Daedriel. The pair of white wings glistened with a pink hue from the setting sun. "Did you know you have an interesting neighbor? She's human."

"We're on Earth, and humans live here. Aren't you supposed to be watching the energetic screen for any signs of disruption? We have to find Rask and retrieve the Reversal Black Tourmaline."

"I was. But then I heard loud noises in the woods, so I went to check. That's my job, isn't it? I'm supposed to investigate if something doesn't seem normal and notify you."

Daedriel sighed, knowing it could be a long conversation with Tika's ability to talk on and on.

"What did you find out?" Daedriel landed on the balcony of his house and folded back his wings. The modern home was built by an architect and contained all the amenities that were useful for Daedriel. He'd spent an obscene amount of money on the purchase. He needed to be at the center of this place where dark energy pulsed strongly. But there was another unidentified source of energy that called to him.

Daedriel shifted his wings into invisible mode and stared at his parrot. "I'm listening. What did you find out? And be quick about it."

"Well, it was nice seeing you too." The parrot gave him a

look similar to an "eye roll." Tika was a celestial creature that could mimic beings around him.

Exhausted from the hunt for Rask, Daedriel wasn't in the mood to chit-chat. He had flown along the eastern coast, trying to locate his enemy. The fact that Rask could've already used that stone infused with dark energy twisted Daedriel's stomach. He didn't want to think about that catastrophe.

But if Rask had used it, Daedriel would have felt the shock waves. The energetic disruption would have interfered with Earth's frequencies. The release of extreme malice and menace from the Reversal Black Tourmaline would open a gateway for more evil to enter and reproduce on Earth at an exponential rate. The dark energy held within this stone came from dangerous beings that wielded potent powers. Darkness existed everywhere. It knew how to maneuver and manipulate energies to suit its needs. The Reversal Black Tourmaline was the steroid needed to empower itself.

Daedriel couldn't let that happen here on Earth—a place already immersed with so much suffering. On a third-dimensional matrix, Earth was more vulnerable than other planets that existed on a higher frequency. Humans who were weak in their minds and hearts would be affected most. The teeth of evil would sink into them, turning them into willing soldiers to expand cruelties.

Damaat. Where the fuck was Rask?

"I'm tired, Tika. I've been searching for the bastard for two days."

The parrot made a sound and jumped onto Daedriel's shoulder. "We'll find him, Dae."

ACKNOWLEDGMENTS

Thank you to Laurie, Carol, and Anna who helped my story shine. You are the shiny siSTARS in my galaxy. Thank you to my family who always give me everything I need to pursue my dreams. You are my entire Universe.

And thank you, dear readers, you give me a reason to keep writing. Without you, there's no one to appreciate the stardust within my creation. You have my utmost gratitude. Thank you, thank you, thank you.

ABOUT THE AUTHOR
CALLA ZAE

Calla Zae writes otherworldly romance. She loves delving into fantastical worlds where her imagination roams wild. Calla is also an artist who enjoys playing with colors, textures, and patterns. She has a love for mysticism, astrology, astronomy, Kdrama, Cdramas, true crime TV shows, romantic suspense novels, cats, and nature.

Calla lives in Massachusetts with her husband who keeps her grounded to Earth and two creative children who think she has her own secret planet. They're onto something...